The Eighteenth Parallel

Ashokamitran (1931–2017) is a pioneer of modern Tamil literature and a towering literary figure, with a prolific career spanning six decades. His published works include a play, eight collections of short stories, eight novels, novellas, besides several edited anthologies, essays, literary criticism and reviews. *Karaintha Nizhalgal* (Star-Crossed, 1969), *Tanneer* (Water, 1973), *Padinettavadu Atchakodu* (*The Eighteenth Parallel*, 1977), and *Indru* (Today, 1984) are among his best known novels.

Ashokamitran had diverse interests, including theatre and film, and served on several film appreciation and certification panels. One of the earliest Tamil authors to write on the conditions of women, he also translated Anita Desai's award-winning novel *Fire on the Mountain* into Tamil, as *Malai Mel Nerruppu*. He received the distinguished Ilakkiya Chintanai awards in 1977 and 1984, and the Government of Tamil Nadu awards for fiction of the year in 1985, 1987 and 1990. His short story collection *Appavin Snegidhar* (*Father's Friend*) won the 1996 Sahitya Akademi Award. His novels and stories have been extensively translated, and his unique prose style left an indelible mark on younger writers.

Gomathi Narayanan is a writer, researcher and translator who has taught at both Kerala and Delhi universities. Her articles and literary translations from Tamil have appeared in the Sahitya Akademi journal *Indian Literature* and other periodicals. Her published works include *Anuvum Namum* (1963), which won the Madras University Award for popular work in the field of science, and *Sahibs and the Natives: A Study of Guilt and Pride in Anglo-Indian and Indo-Anglian Novels* (1986). Other than Ashokamitran's *The Eighteenth Parallel*, her works in translation include *Silent Storm* (1990), a translation of the novel *Mauna Puyal* by Vaasanthi, and *The Guilty and Other Stories* (2002), also by Vaasanthi. She lives in Chennai where she also teaches part-time.

The Eighteenth Parallel is a work of fiction and as such should not be seen to present authentic history, notwithstanding the mention of some historical persons and events.

The Eighteenth Parallel

ASHOKAMITRAN

Translated from the original Tamil by

GOMATHI NARAYANAN

Orient BlackSwan

THE EIGHTEENTH PARALLEL

ORIENT BLACKSWAN PRIVATE LIMITED

Registered Office
3-6-752 Himayatnagar, Hyderabad 500 029, Telangana, India
e-mail: centraloffice@orientblackswan.com

Other Offices
Bengaluru, Chennai, Guwahati, Hyderabad, Kolkata, Mumbai, New Delhi, Noida, Patna, Visakhapatnam

Originally published in Tamil as *Padinettavadu Atchakodu* (Chennai: Kalaignan Pathippakam, 1977)

The Eighteenth Parallel first published by Disha Books, Orient Blackswan Private Limited 1993
Second edition 2023

038080

ISBN 978-93-5442-449-6

Typeset in
Palatino Linotype 11/13
by Le Studio Graphique, Gurgaon 122 007

Printed in India at
Thomson Press, New Delhi 110 020

Published by
Orient Blackswan Private Limited
3-6-752 Himayatnagar, Hyderabad 500 029, Telangana, India
e-mail: info@orientblackswan.com

To my sons
Ravi, Muthu and Ramakrishnan
for always placing my pursuit
before their interests

'You mean to say the Nizam who was crowned today asked you to give me these seven rotis?'

'Yes, holy one. He chose them himself.'

The Sufi mystic's eyes narrowed for a moment. 'How generous! How charitable of him to give me this shrivelled-up bread, no better than dried leaves! What a pity! His line will dry up with the seventh generation.'

Traditional story from the Deccan,
eighteenth century

'Is Hyderabad a leasehold of the Government of India? It is a quirk of history that the jailbirds of yesterday should now be harassing princes of noble lineage. Here in Hyderabad we have a royal line of three centuries blessed by Allah. The atrocities of the rogue Indian government can't go on for long. The foamy waves of the Bay of Bengal shall soon caress the feet of our beloved Rustom-i-Dewan, Arastu-i-Zamon, Lt General, Muzaffar-al-Mulk, Wal-Mumaik, Fateh Jung Sippah Salaar Mir Usman Ali Khan Bahadur Nizam-ul-Mulk, Asaf Jah, G.C.S.I., G.C.B.E. The waters of the Arabian Sea shall wet the golden sandals of our beloved Nizam. The sacred Asaf Jahi flag shall fly over the ramparts of the Red Fort at Delhi.'

A Razakar speech (1948)

1

'We have net practice today, dost,' said Nasir Ali Khan. 'Zaroor ajana.' Nasir Ali Khan, the captain designate of the college cricket eleven, had even made it to the Moinuddaula Cup team which bristled with senior players and, going in to bat as the tenth man, had pulled off a thirty-three not out in barely ten minutes. Out of the four hundred students in Chandru's college, just about forty had ventured into cricket. And none had any doubt that Nasir would be captain, not just that year but as long as one could foresee. And here was Nasir, the boy who wore a silk shirt and flannel trousers even at practice, mind you; here he was, inviting Chandru to the net! Considering that the chances of a Khan getting to hear about a Chandrasekharan were rather thin. As soon as Nasir left, Chandru shot to the bicycle stand and squeezed the tyres to check them. Good, they were both full.

As it happened, both the hours that afternoon went to chemistry practicals, luckily. One good thing about practicals was that students were not required to stay on until the session ended. Your experiment done, you were well rid of the teacher, and free to leave. Chandru took the solution he'd been given in a test tube and made a few visits to the hydrogen sulphide chamber to let the gas bubble through the solution, a preliminary test to determine the salt group.

The solution turned dark every time. A confirmatory test would now be required to ascertain the exact metallic constituent. In an earlier class he'd been given barium. Guessing what it was this time shouldn't prove too difficult as there were twenty pairs of students doing their practicals that afternoon, and at least half a dozen were sure to get it right. Once *they* had the answer, the rest of the class would have an easy time of it.

At half-past three, Chandru had already gathered up his books and was headed in the direction of the bicycle stand, only to be stopped by the old man who was in charge there. 'No, you can't take it out now,' he said.

'Look, there's cricket practice today,' said Chandru, 'I need to rush home and rush back.'

'Well you can't have your bicycle. Come back at four for it.'

Chandru glared at the old man, no more than five feet in shabby pyjamas and shirt. The shirt hung loosely down to his knees. Grey moustache, grey beard. At least four teeth were missing. His cheeks had withered and collapsed with this and the bidis he constantly smoked. His eyes were two dull glass marbles. It wasn't as if he was not in the habit of salaaming everyone. Not at all. He would wipe your bicycle clean. Oil your bicycle. Fill air in your tyres. Look after your books. Fetch a betel-leaf bida or cigarettes for you. Push your car if you had trouble starting. All you needed to make him grovel at your feet was a fair skin. It certainly helped if you wore tweed, spoke Urdu and answered to names which had a noble ring—Khan, Ali or Ahmad.

Chandru gave the old man two annas which was what he had at the time. The man now moved aside to let him in and stood looking away while the bicycle was wheeled out, as if it had nothing to do with him.

A five minutes' ride and Chandru was at the Husain Sagar lake. And now the Tank Bund—a whole mile of embankment road stretched straight ahead. A sharp wind blew on the bund adjoining the lake, though the lake itself appeared deceptively calm.

Riding against the wind, eyes bloodshot and streaming, Chandru still found the Tank Bund exhilarating. It was a dam-like granite structure topped with concrete, smooth and straight with cast iron railings, and it ran for a mile along one side of the lake. There were three balcony-like structures jutting out onto the lake. How pleasant it would be to sit there in the evenings! But then that would mean cycling three miles from home. He couldn't afford the bus, not till he grew up and earned his living, all rather too far in the future. But why not spend five minutes here today? On his way back from cricket maybe?

'Back from college already?' asked his mother. Chandru didn't speak. He just went on to open his box and took out a pair of white trousers.

'Oh it's cricket I see.'

Again, Chandru did not reply.

'But you said some boys attacked you on the playground the other day,' Mother persisted.

'But today's practice is in our college.'

'Don't tell me you're going back to college now.'

'Yes, I am.'

'In that case, bring the buffalo back home before you go. The boy's forgotten to tie it up.'

That galvanised Chandru. He bolted through the back door, and was sprinting in no time at all across a large open field towards a group of buildings—a church and a row of four large bungalows. Last week, the boy they had engaged to put their water-buffalo to graze had done the same thing. He had left the animal unsecured. And the crooked-horned creature had strayed into the church gardens. The gardener had caught it, thrashed it soundly, and then taken it to a pound three miles away. Two days and two sleepless nights of frantic search followed. And a fine of three rupees. All through this the gardener never breathed a word about his part in the affair. When questioned later, he had said, 'Next time I'll hack it to bits.'

So the first thing Chandru did now was to look round the church premises. Crooked Horns wasn't there. Lucky. But was it really? What if the wretched creature had wandered off to somewhere worse than the church?

Back home again.

'Amma, you always seem to wait till I'm in a breathless hurry,' said Chandru, 'and then you send me on some awkward errand.' His mother dropped the dosai turner into a trough of water. That was supposed to bring lost cattle home. Chandru went out on his bicycle.

He pedalled slowly round the bungalows, scanning the gardens from the outside. Then he spotted the animal. It had come to a dreadful place indeed, a place strictly out of bounds, for the name plate outside proclaimed—'Mohd Kasim. Hyderabad Police'. In the garden the buffalo was enjoying an easeful repast of some of this gentleman's well-tended potted crotons.

Chandru leaned his bicycle against the wall, and went in through the open gate, walking on his toes. He tried to pull the buffalo by the horns but the animal impudently ignored him. Then he picked up a stone and flung it at the animal from behind. The buffalo now took off at a gallop, knocking down the flower pots and streaking through the gate in a flash. Another moment and Chandru would have made it too, but as luck would have it he found himself in the grip of a policeman who was supposed to have guarded the place all the time but had failed to do so.

Chandru pleaded for mercy. 'Please sir, be kind enough to forgive me sir,' he said. The constable surveyed the trail of havoc left by the buffalo and grabbed Chandru's shirt. Chandru abjectly repeated his entreaties. Just then a woman, very fat, very short and very fair, appeared on the scene and let out a torrent of choice Urdu abuse at the constable. Then, she began to wander round the garden muttering. 'The ass, the swine, the ass, the swine....' The policeman followed her meekly. Chandru stood there not quite sure what he should do, but as soon as the two disappeared behind the building, he shot out through the gate. He found the buffalo on a slow march homeward and accompanied it on his bicycle. Now on her best behaviour, Crooked Horns went straight to her shed and stood there patiently waiting to be tied to the stake. Chandru fastened the free end of the rope round her neck. Then he picked up a stout wedge of firewood.

'Oh no, don't! Don't!' cried his mother. 'She's just a poor dumb creature, Chandru, please don't beat her,' till Chandru finally threw the stick down and swore at the buffalo. 'You wretched animal, you Sani!' Then he ran into the house and started to put on his white shirt and trousers.

'You'd better have something to eat before you go,' said Mother. 'You have such a long way to ride and for the second time today.'

'To hell with eating! I don't want anything.' Chandru pulled on his cricket shoe.

'Some tea then?'

'Well, why don't you bring it?' Chandra shouted. 'Do you expect me to linger around at home forever?'

It was at this point that Chandru's sisters and his little brother Pitchumani returned from school. Pitchumani leapt on to Chandru's other shoe and began to try it on. Chandru dealt him a sharp slap which set him screaming.

'Now, Chandru,' his mother protested, 'what are you raising the roof for? What's the matter with you?'

'Sani! That's what. Curse my wretched Sani-smitten bad luck.' Then he darted to his bicycle, his second shoe unlaced, and was out in no time at all.

'That's right,' Mother was saying, 'you're well and truly in Sani's bane.' She was merely quoting the astrologer. It appeared that the malevolent Sani was on the ascent in Chandra's horoscope and would continue his calamitous reign for seven and a half years, of which only four months had passed. For that matter, the astrologers themselves were very much in the ascendancy in Chandru's house in recent times. Nothing unusual in a family with daughters to marry.

There wasn't much of a wind against him on the Tank Bund this time. The Husain Sagar lake seemed to defy the laws of nature. The wind always blew against you, at least some of it, no matter which direction you took. This light breeze would make for a really pleasant bus ride. But buses from Secunderabad plied only once every half hour. And only from the railway station which was more than a mile from home. Anyhow, there was no point going by bus if he wanted to be on time for cricket practice which was from four-thirty to six. One had to think of the expense as well—six annas. If only they could get a house closer to college. But Father's quarters were meant to be close to his work place, the railway administrative offices. The place Chandru's family were occupying had been their home for years now. They had filled it up with a sizeable collection of lumber, the kind you invariably accumulated if you stayed in the same house for long.

The last lap of his ride. Just a furlong to go. Of the five miles between home and college, it was this mile-long stretch of the Bund, free of buildings and shops, with the lake on one side and a drop of more than twenty feet on the other, that had always fascinated him. Every inch of it.

Chandru didn't really expect to play well at practice today. How could he after this hectic ten mile ride in a single hour with the added frenzy of a buffalo chase thrown in? Worse, he had had no tea or tiffin. He had hopes of getting into Team B even if denied a place on Team A, but it all depended on his putting in some regular practice this week. To think that he who had been a captain of sorts was now to play under someone else. Who was the Team B captain? Whoever it was, wasn't it futile to expect him to make allowances? Chandru was not one of those who was in fine form from the start. He needed a couple of overs in which to warm up before he could bowl well. To make matters worse, the captain would speak in Urdu and only Urdu. Chandru could just about manage the language, he could never hope to communicate anything smartly in it. Things would be different, though, with Nasir Ali Khan. He would understand. He must have heard about Chandru, surely, or he wouldn't have bothered to invite him personally. Why should the boy choose today of all days to let the buffalo stray? And send him to play cricket on an empty stomach. Blame it all on Sani, the seven-and-a-half-year Sani. He was troubled with a vague sense of doom and wondered if his cricketing days, days of games and play, would last much longer.

He left the Tank Bund behind, turned into a street and cycled past the Rose Biscuit Factory. About fifty people had assembled on the open grounds of the factory. Tall–short, thin–fat, old–young, they were a most mixed crowd in their pyjamas and shirts, trousers, sherwani jackets, whatever. But each of them had a bamboo stick aslant their shoulders, like a rifle at slope arms. An official from the Hyderabad Police or the army was also there instructing them.

It was with an uneasy feeling that Chandru remembered that this was exactly what was happening on the grounds near his house where his cricket group had been playing for years. Recently, the field had been taken over by similar men on a similar mission. And Hyderabad and Secunderabad had also suddenly filled up with unfamiliar faces. Small tin and bamboo shanties overflowing with people had suddenly sprung up on both sides of Station Road in Secunderabad. His father and uncle said that hundreds more like them waited on the platforms of Kazipet railway station. It appeared that they were converging to Hyderabad from places around the state. Some had come from Nagpur and nearby places. They were poor. Muslims, but poor. Once you left the Tank Bund and entered Hyderabad city you found the streets swarming with these outsiders. One look at them and you knew they were not from Hyderabad. In a grim situation like this, cricket and the rest would soon be an anomaly. Yet, the fact remained that he had been invited by Nasir Ali Khan. Did Nasir go to arms-train? Did even rich people's sons, sons of the high like Nasir, put on baggy pyjamas and go marching with a bamboo stick for a gun?

Not that Chandru was averse to marching himself. In fact, he had wanted to join the Auxiliary Corps when he entered college last year, but was rejected after being found underweight by four pounds. This year the corps was open to anyone who was interested. But then this year, ever since the college had reopened after the summer holidays, the air had been fraught with conflict because, while the whole of India was looking forward to August 1947 and Independence,

Hyderabad sought something else. It did not want to join the Indian Union. Some other princely states were preparing to declare their independence too. Travancore and Junagadh were not going to accede to India. Neither was Kashmir. There had been riots in Travancore and Sir CP had been stabbed in the face. Sir CP who? Sir CP, Dewan and Chief Advisor to the Maharaja of Travancore. The other Hyderabad, the one in Sind, had gone to Pakistan. But this one, the Deccan Hyderabad, aspired to be an independent sovereign state. Then there had been the Hindu-Muslim riots countrywide. Five hundred butchered in Bengal, five thousand in Bihar and fifty thousand in Punjab. And then it was midnight, August 14. Chandru and the whole family crowded round their decrepit radio. The Union Jack was being lowered and the Indian tricolour hoisted, all to the accompaniment of atmospherics—salutations to the motherland! Long live India! Vande Mataram! Jai Hind! *krkrkrkrkrkrkr...* Now switch it off. Can't hear a thing. Better be careful, son. August is when Sani starts his seven and a half year's reign. These are bad times, going from bad to worse. This is no time for your cricket and all that. You have to be careful...

Chandru had managed the Bund without much effort, but the slope near Bashir Bagh found him out of breath. With just fifty yards to go, he was straining every muscle. It must be past four-thirty now. He didn't know for certain, he had no watch. Father wouldn't buy him one yet—'I bought you a bicycle last year, didn't I?' But buying a bicycle for him last year had actually meant a saving of six annas a day, ten rupees a month. And the cost of a new one? Just a hundred and thirty rupees for a 'war quality' bicycle. They sold war quality bicycles in Hyderabad though it was two years since the World War had ended and India had become free. Freedom hadn't come to Hyderabad though. Only vast hordes of immigrants. If these people actually undertook to live in these hovels with occasional practice drills and bamboos for rifles, the life they had left behind must have been terrible indeed. Wasn't there a special name for them? Ah yes, refugees. Re-fyu-jee, was that how you spelt it? Must look up the dictionary.

Chandru pedalled furiously in through the college gate. The playground wasn't yet visible. Once he crossed the Science Block, the grounds came into view. Also a few heads, but not on the near side. The boys were all on the far side of the ground where a practice net had been provided. Chandru had been there only a few times last year, and that as an onlooker. He had even watched Nasir Ali Khan play. Today, for the first time, he was going to play there as an accredited player of the college. He made a detour to the other side of the ground as cycling was prohibited on the playfield and found that a sizeable crowd had collected there. Was it always crowded there, he wondered, or was it because it was the first day of the season. If he were to wait until all of them had had a turn, at the net, it would be well past seven. Maybe he wouldn't get a chance to play at all today. But then he'd come late and had no right to grumble. All because that boy had let the buffalo loose. It could, of course, have been worse. The buffalo had somehow been found, thank God, or he wouldn't be here at all.

The look that Nasir Ali Khan gave Chandru was not the friendliest. Sundar Singh was there. So were Nizam Yar Khan and several others whose faces were familiar but whose names were not. These boys had high-schooled at the Madras-e-Aliya, the school for princes, right there on the college campus, a school run specially for the sons of nobility. Two of the Nizam's grandsons were in the school now. For boys such as these, college did not mean a break from school. They all wore white shirts and trousers and cricket shoes. A boy from the history department was batting now. Three boys bowled to him in turn so that there was no break in the bowling, and they had three balls to bowl with.

Nasir said, 'You're very late, dost,' but he didn't look cross at all. Then he picked up a ball and handed it to

Chandru. Chandru hesitated for a moment, then he returned it. 'I'd rather not bowl today,' he said.

Nasir passed the ball on to someone else. He said something to Chandru which he didn't quite catch. He had already resigned himself to an evening of nothing but fielding. Nasir repeated what he said, this time in English. 'I said pad up.' Chandru was taken aback. He picked up a pair of pads from the cricket gear piled there and buckled them on to his legs. Then he chose a bat, the best seeming of the lot, and stood waiting his turn. Most of the players must have felt that the captain unduly favoured the newcomer. Just arrived, and he gets a chance to bat already!

2

Before I embark on a history of my cricket, let me tell you something about the place we lived in. Moving house was an annual ritual with us until I was twelve. It was then that we finally settled down in a house which, unlike the ones we had lived in until then, was situated quite far from the centre of the town. A mile or a bit more lay between us and the railway station, the market and the nearest school. The fact of the matter was that my father had at last been allotted government quarters. The place was called Lancer Barracks. At first I found this name with its faint ring of a swear word an embarrassment. A vast stretch of rugged terrain, more than ten acres, with a three-foot brick wall to mark off its boundaries and two long tile-roofed structures in the middle, each partitioned into twelve sections one behind the other, thus making twenty-four houses in all—well that was Lancer Barracks for you.

Although I can't say for sure when these barracks were built, there's one thing I know. They were meant for giants ten foot tall. You had to stand on a chair or a stool to fasten the top bolts of the doors. The roof must have been a good twenty-five feet at its peak from where it sloped down on either side. The walls couldn't have been an inch less than two feet thick. Just to look up at the roof in half-light gave one the shivers.

I found out the following from the dictionary:

> **lancer:** a soldier of a cavalry regiment armed with lances
> **barrack:** permanent building(s) in which soldiers are lodged

Lancer Barracks must therefore have been built for the British soldiers armed with lances. I wondered if these soldiers were expected to carry their lances all the time. Quite likely. And their lances must have been rather long. Perhaps that explained why they needed such high roofs. The lances would otherwise have scraped the roofs. These barracks must somehow have come into the possession of the Railway Department and been converted into living quarters for their employees. And here was my father, settled at last in this haven. It turned out he had waited fifteen whole years to move into these houses.

For that matter, all the other occupants of Lancer Barracks had been on the waiting list equally long before they were allotted houses there. Our line of barracks housed two Tamil families including ours, three Anglo-Indians, four Muslims, one Parsi and two Naidus. There was only one Tamil family in the row behind ours. The rest were again Anglo-Indians, Parsis, Muslims and Naidus. The Naidus had me speculating. Could it be that all those who spoke Telugu were called Naidus?

Our barracks, as I said, was quite far from the city, though there were a few buildings even beyond ours. There was a church and a few small houses in a large compound next to ours. Further afield were four large bungalows in a row. A Christian cemetery lay separated from the church by half a mile. None of us had ever seen this cemetery being used. The gravestones and memorial slabs were thickly overgrown with weeds. My little brother and I sometimes climbed over the wall and explored the place, our hearts racing. Most of the graves belonged to the nineteenth century, though an occasional tombstone spoke of the twentieth, and all the dead had been in the British army. Apparently soldiers had died in large numbers in our barracks, which meant that they had lived there in large numbers to begin with. Some of the inscriptions had more than thirty names. All fallen in battle perhaps, or fallen prey to the plague or smallpox which were endemic to Hyderabad-Secunderabad in those times. But for our barracks, the church, the row of bungalows and the cemetery, this stretch of country was deserted, rugged moorland. There were a few hills and hillocks in the far distance. It was a place for ghosts rather than humans. It wasn't a bad place for grazing cattle though.

Now, there was no dearth of wide open spaces within our barracks compound, but very little of it was level ground and the only stretch that was somewhat even had already been appropriated by the adults for badminton. And so when Santanam and I went looking for a pitch for our first ever game of cricket, we had to be happy with a patch of bumpy ground, comparatively less up and down than the rest. Santanam, you see, was the boy from the last house in our row. He was in my class and like me, he had a younger brother. I had sisters who were both older and younger, but Santanam had only a brother. Only the three of us—Santanam, his brother and I—played cricket. My brother was too young for the game.

We drew vertical lines on the walls for our wicket. A strip of wooden board served us for a bat, and our ball was a tennis ball. These descriptions can be quite misleading, I know. In case you've gained the impression of many years of cricket played this way, let me hasten to set the record straight—we played this sort of cricket for no more than two months at the most.

Though we were only three players, we drew lots as to who should begin: Number 1 or Number 2. Santanam's brother was the permanent third man. When Santanam won the draw and went in to bat first, his innings would be over in half an hour. If I batted first, however, we would still be playing to the end of the day with the end of the game nowhere in sight. This is not to say that I played exceedingly well. Rather, it could be put down to the quality of Santanam's bowling.

A map of India would be useful to illustrate Santanam's bowling graphically. As you know, Delhi is due north of Secunderabad. Imagine me then batting from Delhi. Secunderabad is the other end of the pitch that Santanam is bowling off. Santanam's run up was an outrageously long affair. When he finally did release the ball, it would take off east towards Calcutta or west towards Karachi, never north to me. He favoured Karachi mostly, perhaps owing to some built-in bend in his physique. To hit the ball, I had to chase it all the way to Karachi. Then the ball would soar in the direction of the African continent, and Santanam would begin to haul his brother over the coals: 'Here I am, straining every nerve, bowling my life away, and there you stand rooted to the ground. Can't you do some fielding, you fool?' He didn't seem to care about my predicament of having to bat my life away after his bowling. It was beyond the realm of possibility that his ball should ever strike those black coal lines that served for wicket. The only way then to dismiss me was to catch me out. A catch was a catch even if the ball struck the ground before it was caught. Actually, it qualified for a catch even if the ball had been pitched a number of times. Our game had only a vague resemblance to cricket. Santanam's long pre-bowling sprint followed by my running after his ball, followed still later by Santanam's brother's run in a third direction to retrieve the ball—it was altogether more like a track event. Only, instead of starting simultaneously, the runners ran in sequence. True, I found Santanam's Karachi-ward bowling extremely irksome, but I wouldn't have stopped playing with him for just that. There were other reasons why we couldn't continue for long, namely, the other boys in Lancer Barracks.

There were ten or fifteen Muslim and Anglo-Indian boys in our own line of the barracks, but my problem was that I couldn't speak their languages, Urdu and English. Santanam and I became play companions mainly because he was a Tamil boy like me, and like me, he spoke no Urdu or English. For the first two days our strange cricket proceeded without a hitch. Then, the Anglo-Indian boys along with the Muslim boys started to watch our game, sitting on the compound wall of the barracks. They found every bit of our show uproariously funny. Santanam's tortuously long run, my pursuit of the ball, the loud abuses showered on Santanam's brother—everything was a rare treat for them. It has to be said that I would have found it a rare treat too if I'd been sitting with them. They would yell 'Bomman! Bomman!' at us. Anyone who spoke a different language was a bomman. Santanam was 'Bada Bomman' and I was 'Chota Bomman'. As the jeers rose higher and higher, Santanam's performance plummetted to new depths until even I, who had never protested until then, shouted at him—'Try to bowl straight, will you?' To which he replied, 'Don't you see me bowling my life away?' But the more he stepped up his efforts in this 'bowling-unto-death', the greater was the harassment from the Anglo-Indian boys, mainly Morris. Morris was the resident bully who even dared to smoke within the barracks premises. Morris would imitate Santanam; he would twist himself into knots and bowl a stone at me. One day he snatched the ball from Santanam and bowled it himself. As if on cue, the other boys ran in and tried to snatch the batting board from me. I raced round the barracks, but the boys were bigger and had little trouble wrenching it from me. Then they started to play. I must admit though that they played a better game than we did.

For a few days Santanam and I played where they couldn't get at us. But a game like cricket is not easy to conceal. Finally, our bat and ball were confiscated by Morris' group. The bat didn't last long under Morris' savage strokes.

Santanam came home and threatened me—I must replace the bat or else he would ask his father to beat up my father. I would ask my father, I said, to kick his father. Our fathers never ever came to blows, but that marked the end of my relationship with Santanam. After that day we never spoke to each other, though we continued to be neighbours for several years. In fact, I didn't see Santanam play any game after that. He started to wear spectacles. That could have been one of the reasons why he didn't play, though there could be several others.

Unlike Santanam, I found it impossible not to play. I joined the Anglo-Indian boys in their games of marbles, monkeys-on-trees and tip-cat. I went with Morris to every Tarzan film that came to town. I swung through the aerial roots of the two banyan trees in Lancer Barracks with a jungle yell like Johnny Weismuller's. And sometimes I played badminton and carrom with the adults.

Two new factors now emerged on the scene to effectively dampen the exuberance of those times. The first was a she-buffalo we bought; the second was the boys of a Tamil family which lived in the second row of Lancer Barracks.

It was not as if Father had ever wanted to buy a water buffalo. It so happened that he once gave our milkman Chotu a loan of sixty rupees of which he barely managed to collect fifteen. Chotu disappeared shortly after that, but presumably on his instructions, his wife brought us an old water buffalo, hitched it to our gate and left. Within the next half hour, the buffalo had moved on with the gate in tow. Father and I went round asking if anyone had seen a buffalo with a gate attached to it. Most people found the question a little beyond their comprehension. Then followed a wide-ranging search which led us to the church compound, and we entered it for the first time in our lives. We were given our buffalo back along with some advice from the padre that a rumbustious beast like ours was not meant to be hitched to a gate. After a great deal of trouble, we managed to drag the animal home and shut it up in our bathroom. 'Ayyayyo!' cried Mother in panic, 'We forgot to take the boiler out!'

'A water buffalo is not likely to eat your boiler,' Father pointed out.

The mooing set in at three in the morning. The buffalo hadn't been fed or milked the evening before. Even Father must have had second thoughts about his remarks concerning the boiler. The man who brought us our milk said he didn't know how to milk a buffalo. Father was afraid even to open the bathroom door, but then the daily habits of a household couldn't be postponed indefinitely. It was Mother who finally let the buffalo out, and eventually milked it too.

The addition of a water buffalo to our household effected a drastic change in our eating habits. It dropped down generous quantities of dung which we learnt to collect into heaps once we'd overcome our initial disgust. Mother acquired milking skills without any instruction or training, and I followed after as the oldest child of the family.

For quite some time, we didn't give the animal a name. We began to feel rather guilty about this, particularly because the milk had greatly enhanced the quality of the coffee at home. We began to call her Lakshmi. This caused many jokes to be made about us. Imagine calling a buffalo—a buffalo, mind you, not a cow—after the goddess of wealth! Meanwhile, the animal was shaping nicely in her new surroundings and was beginning to take liberties. She would climb the half-dozen steps that led from the kitchen to the backyard and eat the blackgram dal and rice left soaking to be ground for dosais. This was easily forgiven. Not so the other predilection she had of snapping herself free of the stake and visiting the church, thus sorely trying the padre's principles of Christian charity. The name Lakshmi soon yielded place to 'Crooked Horns', which stuck.

We employed a boy to take Crooked Horns to graze near the hillock. The grass was thin in these parts and fodder had to be bought. Hay was not to be had as this was not paddy country. Only guinea grass and maize stalks were available. The grass could be fed to the animal as it was, but the stalks had to be chopped up. Since Lancer Barracks was very far from the city, the grass carters did not come there often, which meant that we had to buy in great quantities when they did, and we needed to have a good store of fodder at home. Despite all our care, emergencies such as not having a blade of grass in the manger, were not uncommon. A frugal feed would tell at once on the girth of the animal, and there she would stand, restless and flustered, the pathetic moistness of her translucent eyes making you want to look away. Whenever Crooked Horns went without her feed, we—Father, Mother and I—ate little and slept even less. We would wait all day in the hope of seeing a grass cart. If it didn't turn up, I would ride two miles to Monda and carry back twenty-five bundles of grass. Twenty-five bundles didn't last more than half an hour for the buffalo, but that was all I could fetch on my small bicycle. It was impossible to persuade any grass carter to come home because they were reluctant to come a whole three miles on the strength of a boy's word. Now the changes effected by the buffalo and its successors—buffaloes, cows and calves—on this chapter of my life which I might call playdays would require some telling indeed. Summing it up in a few words is impossible. Briefly, a water buffalo was trying its best, unwittingly of course, to dislodge an international game from my consciousness where Santanam had placed it. There were those young scions of a Tamil family in Lancer Barracks, Krishnaswamy and his two younger brothers who, together with the buffalo, robbed me of much of the joy of playtime during my school days. I owed them my first serious thoughts of murder and suicide.

Krishnaswamy's house was the last in the second row of houses in Lancer Barracks just as mine was the last in the first row. His father wore a white uniform and took a train every second day—whether as a guard or a ticket-examiner, I couldn't say for certain. Anyway, in my eyes, he was a very high official. Krishnaswamy was older than me and was my senior at school. Balu, the first of his younger brothers, was in my class but in another section. The youngest, Goku, was in the next lower class. The brothers' sing-song speech with no final elisions sounded curiously precise. People from Palghat in Kerala spoke Tamil with this special accent, my mother said.

The person I came across most was Balu. In school, Balu was like any other Tamil boy among the hundreds of Telugu and Muslim boys, a lost sheep. But when he had his brothers with him, he was a terror.

How the whole thing began eludes my memory, but Balu and I had somehow become 'enemies'. Once this 'enemy' status was formalised, Balu started to both come to school and go back with his brothers. One evening, on my way home, the three brothers walked beside me and kept nudging and jostling me to the edge of the road. First to the foot-track along the road, then to the verge overgrown with thorny bushes, and finally into the ditch. Since our city never got much rain, and there was no traffic on the road, I just got up from the dry ditch, dusted off my shirt and shorts and began to walk again, taking care to keep a good fifty yards behind them. But a tiger that has tasted blood once must of necessity taste it again. Krishnaswamy and his brothers pushed me into the ditch a second time. I was still alone but not entirely unprepared this time. I scratched Krishnaswamy and Balu on their faces. That was the end of the fight for the day.

I didn't attract much attention at home as a rule. But now glances of suspicion began to spring out at me. In the mornings, I would get ready quickly and start out for school at nine, which was much too early. In the evenings, I would be home within ten minutes of closing time, all this in an effort to avoid Krishnaswamy and his brothers on the road. Escaping them in the morning wasn't too difficult, but the evenings posed a problem because school was out at the same time for everyone and the front gate was never opened before the bell rang. You could try as hard as you could to squeeze your way through the milling crowd at the gate, but it wasn't easy to avoid students who were going the same way as you were. So I began to avoid the main gate altogether. Instead I clambered up the school wall at a lonely spot and climbed over it. This way, I managed to leave school a couple of minutes ahead of my enemies. Soon, a sizeable group of boys began to follow my example. It wasn't long before I took to climbing over the wall even to get to class in the mornings. I began to jump out and hurry away compulsively, even when it was not strictly necessary, as on those days when the dreadful three were absent from school. I used to be in a constant state of alert those days, a fact which didn't escape the family, particularly my mother, for long. Mother told Father, and Father asked what the matter was. I said nothing, not even after the beating I got from him. This was because I felt Krishnaswamy and his brothers were *my* problem and it was for me to tackle them in my own way. But I had no idea how.

I drew up elaborate plans. One was to get hold of the brothers one by one, stuff them into boxes, transport them by rail upto Bombay and finally put them on a boat to Africa. Murder was not an integral part of these detailed and meticulously drawn schemes, but I was quite prepared to handle incidental death. I had a contingency plan for the disposal of the bodies and the stuffing of their clothes up the ship's chimneys and so on. Occasionally, I wondered if it would be better to wait for twenty or thirty years and plot revenge in the tradition of the Count of Monte Cristo rather than mete out immediate retribution. The trouble was that this scheme called for my incarceration in the dungeons of an island prison in which I would dig a tunnel in order to reach a fellow prisoner. An escape from prison, the acquisition of a large hidden treasure followed by several more exploits incognito, these were all essential. I thus lived simultaneously in two worlds. The real world where I was in constant dread of the Krishnaswamy brothers, and the imaginary scenario of the nineteenth-century novels where intrepid exploits were always possible.

There were times when all my schemes appeared futile and impracticable. It was at such times that my thoughts turned to suicide. How did one organise a suicide? Was it possible to commit suicide without anyone's guessing that it was one? Yes. Only, my body should not be seen by anyone. And how could that be managed? Bury it, of course. For this part of my plan I chose the British military cemetery. I took a small crowbar to the cemetery and began to dig in secret. After nearly ten days' digging, I found that I wasn't even a foot deep. The place scared me a bit. Also, the prospect of living with English-speaking ghosts after death wasn't an attractive proposition. So I moved to the foot of the hills in search of a better place for my grave. Opportunities for such investigation offered themselves in plenty once we acquired that water buffalo. On the pretext of looking for the buffalo, I explored the hillock looking for a cave. My plan was to eat poison and die at home, then bring my body myself and secret it in some hollow. A place sufficiently pleasing to my fancy never presented itself, but during these trips I accumulated a fund of knowledge about the place for miles around. I could now divine with reasonable accuracy the hideouts of scorpions which abounded in the red earth. I knew exactly which stone to move to uncover a few. But the creatures seemed so utterly defenceless and miserable when their shelter was disturbed that after the first few times I gave up.

It was then that Santanam entered the scene. It was brought home to me quite early in our acquaintance that in the matter of tackling the Krishnaswamy brothers, Santanam was not to be relied on. One evening, emboldened by the presence of Santanam with me on the road, I walked at a more moderate pace than usual. Finding me within reach after a long time, Krishnaswamy came up and knocked me down. Santanam was the first to charge away, before I could. I never brought up the subject of his desertion with

Santanam. In point of fact, it was after this incident that we began to play cricket. The game was the only link between us. Soon, even that link was broken.

I slowly got used to the loneliness of living with people who spoke alien languages. One reason was that the Anglo-Indian and Muslim boys of Lancer Barracks accepted me as one of them. They used to kill garden lizards. Their speech was generously sprinkled with swear-words. It was swear-this and swear-that all the time—tripping on a stone, losing a game of tip-cat or tops, climbing a tree or passing a cow. If you stood in a queue at the Plaza cinema for a John Hall—Maria Montez film and didn't get a ticket, that also merited a wholesome swear-word. Morris freely used these words to indicate any disagreement with his many brothers and sisters. He had three sisters, two of them older, and all of them flung these words around with ease. The eldest sister was a little restrained in her use of such ammunition, though.

This sister was the only one in Morris' family who was somewhat fair. With the advent of the World War and the arrival of the British soldiers in Secunderabad, she metamorphosed into the likes of the women we saw in the English films. Her English, which we normally followed quite well, took on unintelligible accents whenever she spoke to the soldiers. Once, when a soldier called on her at her house, she made me sit beside her and proceeded to kiss me every five minutes throughout the conversation. I wasn't in the least troubled by this, but the soldier looked terrible. His eyes, face, hands and feet were all pink. He was hairy all over and had a foul smell issuing from his mouth, all of which could have led her to hold me as a kind of protective shield. Morris winked at me.

Two more persons now came to live in Krishnaswamy's house, his uncles who had come looking for jobs in Secunderabad. Their Tamil was even rougher than Krishnaswamy's. Almost immediately following their arrival, they got jobs in the ordnance factory. Those days the factory employed anyone who was sixteen and could write a little English. They worked from eight in the morning but went on only till three-thirty in the afternoon. Now that there were five willing players in their family, they formed a cricket group. The harassments that had bedevilled Santanam's and my cricket did not feature with Krishnaswamy since his group had adults.

As for me, I became the darling of the Anglo-Indian families in Lancer Barracks. In the Muslim homes, I was among the few admitted behind the sackcloth screens where I steeled myself to watch without flinching when the chicken was wrung by its neck. I was often to be found at Morris' house at a game of Monopoly with Morris, his elder brother Terence and his sisters. Their parents would be engaged in a drunken brawl throughout in the same room. I learnt all the popular film songs of the day sung by Khurshid, Johra Begum and Noorjahan. After much persuasion, I got Father and Mother to finally let me have pyjamas made. Then, through Janardanam, a Naidu boy, I got to know his brother Sundar, and Sundar's friends Venkat and Appa Rao. I learnt to play carrom with them. They were also obliged to include me in the badminton for the simple reason that the net belonged to me. This net had been lying unused at home, and I had no idea how it came to be there.

The risqué humour and laughter of these Naidu boys were of a different category from Morris' and his Anglo-Indian friends' swear-words. I never felt uneasy with the Anglo-Indians, but the Naidus had me squirming. The worst offender was Venkat. There was a convent close by from where women of all ages, some in skirts and blouses and others in saris, filed past our barracks. Venkat contrived to throw the badminton ball in their direction and would send me to get it. I got my own back the day our buffalo swished him with her dung-soaked tail. It fell to me to carry a bucket of water to him to wash with. When I poured the water on his trousers, it was of course in a more generous quantity than was strictly required by the occasion.

Krishnaswamy and his brothers played cricket near their house with a few more Tamil boys from outside the barracks. I pretended to enjoy the badminton but it went against the grain with me to have to run after the girls and women from the convent just to satisfy Venkat's and Appa Rao's suppressed cravings. Apart from badminton, the only outdoor games open to me were marbles, tip-cat and monkeys-on-the-tree, all of them primitive games, fit for the uncouth when compared with cricket. Whether or not I fully recognised these nice distinctions, they certainly aggravated the supercilious disdain of the Krishnaswamy brothers. There was one occasion when Krishnaswamy fell foul of Morris, Sajad and Wahab, and I had to watch him being rolled in the dust. After that incident, I was careful on my way to and from school.

I'm aware that as I tell you all this, you may get an impression of the passage of years. In fact, these episodes—the buffalo, Morris, the state of war with Krishnaswamy and his brothers, monkeys-on-the-tree, films like *Tarzan's New York Adventures*, Venkat's and Appa Rao's obscene laughter, the search for a grave in the cemetery, exploring the hills for a place of refuge, Morris' eldest sister's advances—all this took place within a short span of time, certainly not more than a year. When I entered the sixth form, the World War had ended. By then, Morris' second sister had also undergone a transformation. The girl was a little dark. And she was large. Her name was Laura. I have for some reason forgotten the eldest sister's name. Try as hard as I might, the name still eludes me. The human mind is still so utterly unreliable. Several years can be rubbed off from your consciousness without the slightest trace, while the tiniest nuances of a random five minutes may be on call instantly as if they were a stretch of eternity. The mind seems to have a special clock and calendar. Or maybe it has neither.

Well, Morris' eldest sister, who had been bubbling over with high spirits all through the war years had now fallen into despondency. The British soldier who had been a frequent visitor till now had stopped visiting her. They had all been hoping that he would marry her and take her away to England. Nothing came of it, and now all she could look forward to was an Anglo-Indian life like any other girl in Secunderabad. She stayed home when we went to the cinema. Only Laura would come with us. We—Morris, his brother Terence and I, together with Laura and sometimes the other younger sister—used to go to the Plaza cinema. The ticket money for the cheapest class for the matinee show was just four annas, but British four annas, which was equal to five annas in Hyderabad's 'halli' currency. If tickets were not available at the Plaza, we moved on to the Tivoli and on the rare occasion when we drew a blank there as well, it was Dreamland. Terence always made a nuisance of himself at the cinema, kicking the chair in front of him with his booted feet, and striking a match and lighting up the moment he lowered himself into a seat. Morris could be equally troublesome but every single act of Terence's had the stamp of the savage on it, which Laura found rather attractive. All of them cold-shouldered me when they were with their Anglo-Indian friends, but when the family was alone, I was accorded the status of an insider. I was Laura's favourite. Her elder sister liked me too, though in a different way. She found my presence comforting somehow. She would take out the English magazines the soldier had given her and explain them to me page by page. One day, while she was doing this, she suddenly stopped in her tracks, broke down sobbing and threw her arms round me. Moved by all this, I began to cry as well. The noise brought Mr Mannas, her father, there and he pushed us off the sofa. Enter the mother. Three or four pictures on the wall were smashed in the fight that ensued between the mother and the father.

There came a time when all these things changed—'changed' is not the word for it; every bit of it just slipped away from my life. Morris, his eldest sister, the large Laura, Terence, Mannas, Mrs Mannas, all of them. Together with the Muslim boys, my Naidu friends, Janardanan, Appa

Rao, the lot. And something else came to pass, something that had seemed most unlikely. I became a close friend of Krishnaswamy and his brothers!

Ranga Ramanujan deserves credit for this.

Well, now I have heard it said that my father suffered a big loss when the Arbuthnot Bank collapsed. For a long time afterwards, he was often accosted by people with a 'What absolute idiocy, putting your money there!' I also saw some people commiserating with him. 'Poor man, he seems to have lost everything.' What my father had lost was eight hundred rupees, roughly the equivalent of fifty gold sovereigns in those days. By a stroke of coincidence it turned out that the Arbuthnot Bank a thousand miles away, had crashed at the same time as my father was returning from the tailor's with two newly sewn alpaca coats. The strange simultaneity condemned the unlucky coats to limbo for years. It was during my cricket days with Santanam that Father retrieved them for use. For several years after that, these two jackets were in constant use, worn on alternate days. They looked a shiny green one minute and turned a dazzling purple the next. Green, purple, green, purple, green here, purple there. A few places became worn threadbare and began to show patches of scarlet. When they were first taken out after ten years of storage, they were a bit moth-eaten, but otherwise there was no cause for any hesitation or embarrassment in wearing them. The reason lay in a propensity which originated with the tailors of Hyderabad who were conservative to the core. The passage of ten or even twenty years could not make them change their age-old styles. Neither did the general populace find it necessary to change their mode of dress. Schoolboys wore open collar shirts. This style of garment was favoured by most adults as well. It was only if you happened to have some cloth of superior quality or of sufficient length that you went in for a closed collar or 'tie-collar' shirt. Though this ensemble of shirt and trousers permitted of little variation, there were still nuances that gave you a clue to the wearer's communal identity. Muslim boys wore their shirts falling over their shorts, pyjamas or trousers. Among the Tamils who had migrated to Hyderabad, all adults wore the same kind of dress. It was as if they had evolved a uniform by consensus. This comprised a full-sleeved shirt tucked into a dhoti, worn with a coat and a cap. The dhoti was worn with a length of the cloth passing between the legs and separating them. Whatever his caste, Mani *Iyer*, Raghava*chari*, Govindaswami *Naidu* or Pinakapani *Mudaliar*, a Tamil migrant never went out without his regulation headgear. Lawyers and professors sported a turban.

My shorts were always made two inches wider and longer than necessary as I was a 'growing boy'. Even after tightening the buckles to the last possible millimetre, the shorts would be loose at the waist and slip down. To prevent this, I used to roll up the shorts all round the waist, much in the same way that a petticoat or sari is tucked up. This would not show, however, since I wore my shirts falling over my shorts. My tuck-up at the waist also had the incidental advantage of reducing the unwanted length of the shorts. It was on this scene that there now descended two boys whose sole mission in life, for all intents and purposes, was to effect a change in the sartorial habits of the boys of Secunderabad, Raj Kumar and Ranga Ramanujan. Belonging as they did to the new influx into Secunderabad after the end of the war, both these boys had innumerable relatives in the army—a father, a few assorted uncles and brothers.

Raj Kumar wore a new kind of shirt to school which was neither shirt nor coat. The shirt-coat had huge pockets and a stitched-on belt. This garment, Raj Kumar told us, was called a bush coat. Ranga's shirt was open in front and had buttons running up the whole length. While the rest of us had to push our heads through the necks of our shirts, he could put his shirt on like a coat, from the back. This meant that when the process was over, not a hair on his head would be out of place, while we could never get into our shirts without mussing up our hair. Ranga came from a school with a different system of education. Our school authorities must have found themselves in a quandary choosing a class to put him in. After he had sat in a higher class for a few days, he was assigned to our class for a week. He sat bemused throughout the Tamil lesson which went completely over his head. He didn't ever sit a Tamil exam.

One day during Ranga's stint in our class, our English teacher decided to test our grammar. He wrote a long sentence on the blackboard for analysis. Pointing to a part of the sentence he asked, 'What clause is that?' The boys stood up one after the other without answering. Then someone said, 'Noun clause.'

'No, next.'

'Adjectival clause,' ventured another.

'No, next.'

'Adverbial clause,' said the next boy.

These were the only three clauses we'd been taught. The whole class, not just I, was never quite sure which was which. To answer questions on grammar we always depended on our gambling instincts. Now that all these options had been exhausted, we wondered what clause it could be.

The teacher continued to call out 'Next', 'Next', till he came to me.

The teacher now looked like a veritable Shakuni of the Mahabharata, and the class took on the features of the Kaurava assembly. Then I cast the dice.

'Parenthetical clause,' I said.

There was a moment's silence in the class, a deadly silence.

'Next,' called out the teacher. The next boy happened to be Ranga who sat first on the bench behind me. He stood up and said, 'Parenthetical clause.'

At the end of the class the two of us exchanged smiles as befitted two geniuses at English. He wanted to know my name. And I felt the texture of his shirt.

Two days later, Ranga was shifted to the next higher class, to Krishnaswami's section. We didn't speak to each other again until after he finished school and I had also got through my tenth without a hitch, and both of us entered the same college, Nizam College, which was five miles away. Ranga used to come to our barracks to play cricket with Krishnaswami's group, but for all they cared, they may as well have been playing in another country.

The bush coat and the full-open shirt. Soon Secunderabad was also full of them. Tailors charged only a little more for these styles. However when worn with pyjamas these garments posed a problem. If you sat down in a chair, the front ends of the shirts parted to reveal the drawstrings of the pyjamas. A solution was soon found in the shape of pyjamas without drawstrings, a kind of trouserish pyjamas. I too had a pair of these made out of MS 55 cloth which was scarce in Secunderabad at the time. I pestered quite a few people to get this fabric for me. When at last I was able to go about wearing these trouserish pyjamas and a full open shirt, I felt like Janab Jinnah. Jinnah, you see, had the reputation of being the first among the world's best-dressed men.

One day as I was entering Lancer Barracks, Ranga accosted me.

'Which is your house?'

'The last one in the first row,' I said.

As we walked together past Morris' house, his older sister called me. 'Chandru!'

I left Ranga where he was and went in. He couldn't have helped watching Morris' sister talk to me, her hand on my shoulder. She wanted me to get her the latest issue of *Picturegoer*. This British film magazine could only be had from AH Wheeler's at the Secunderabad railway station. It cost four British annas, but Wheeler's sold it at a concession for four annas and four pies of our Hyderabad currency. Morris' sister handed me four annas and four pies.

As I took the coins and made to go, Laura came there looking somewhat larger than usual. Ranga couldn't have helped seeing her either from where he was standing. 'What man, where you going man?' began Laura. All the women in Morris' family ended their sentences with a 'man'. The only exception was Morris' eldest sister. I had the answer to Laura's question in my mind in Tamil, but stood silent unable to decide how to say it in English, 'house' or 'home'. Laura had always taken note of these dilemmas which left me tongue-tied, and found them rather amusing. So she shot another of her questions at me, addressing me again as an adult homo sapien. 'What's blocking that mouth of yours, *man*?' She then pinched both my cheeks, then pulled them apart and looked into my mouth. This again was something Ranga couldn't have missed seeing.

We left Morris' house and started for mine. Just then we had another vision thrown in—Pyari Begum standing outside her house which was next to ours. She was ticket-examiner Kasim's second daughter. In my house they called her fat swine. I had no idea what this animal was. But Pyari Begum looked like a barrel with a sweet face. The final piece of luck, the great attraction, so to speak, was the presence of Nagaratnam in my house. Nagaratnam was my older sister's friend. She was popular among the Tamil families of Secunderabad and took part in the YMCA elocution competitions and danced at school functions. Nagaratnam's tantalising eyes seemed to ask one something. Strangers and acquaintances were fair game alike for her.

And so my stock went up with Ranga. He began to look me up every time he came to play cricket with Krishnaswamy.

For some days Ranga accorded all respect to the strained relations between Krishnaswamy's group and me, and refrained from bringing up the subject. Five or ten minutes was all he could spend at my house before he got bored. Then he would leave for his cricket and I would go looking for Morris, Wahab and the others. But the games I played with them were not the kind which improved with practice, except perhaps tip-cat. Monkeys-on-trees and marbles offered little scope for finesse and didn't sustain my interest for more than a few days.

So when Ranga said one day, 'Why don't you come with me?' I went along. Krishnaswamy and Ranga were the biggest boys in their group apart from the two uncles. These uncles were frequently absent, probably because they felt bored playing with youngsters. The ten or so boys of this group went to a vast open ground half a mile away. They took with them a single pad, a cricket bat, four stumps and an old cricket ball. It was practice cricket every day, with Krishnaswamy and Ranga leading the two sides. I sat under a tree the whole time and Ranga would come and say a few words to me now and again. Krishnaswamy and his brothers kept their aggression towards me in check when they found that Ranga treated me as his equal.

Although the charming Nagaratnam was a frequent visitor to our house and there were some other attractions besides Pyari Begum in the Muslim household next door, and a few things happened which gave people the impression that I was the confidant of all the Anglo-Indian girls in the First Line Barracks, it was soon apparent that none of this was likely to benefit Ranga. For there was this business of the Muslim boys who lived on our first line. They had the habit of calling everyone 'sala'. No utterance of theirs began without a prefatory 'Kya be sala?' This word which connoted a liaison with the addressee's sister was not really applicable to Ranga—he had no sisters. Yet he never failed to bristle at the expression.

I introduced Ranga to Morris and Terence, and we even went to a film at the Tivoli with Laura. It was Ranga who had recommended this particular film, Shakespeare's *Henry V*, with Laurence Olivier in the lead. That is where he went wrong. None of us had reached the stage where we could appreciate Olivier. I myself was an old hand at sitting through a film even if I couldn't understand it. But Terence made a noisy fuss. He blew cigarette smoke on Ranga and me. He also kept up a constant flow of abuse. Laura kept biting into a palm tuber and spitting at the chair in front of her. She would have done it even if the chair had been occupied.

My being friendly with Anglo-Indian boys didn't bother Krishnaswamy much, but in Ranga's case he seemed to have taken some drastic disciplinary measures. One day Ranga gave up cricket and came to play monkeys-on-trees with my group. It fell to his lot to stand at the foot of the tree and protect the stick in front of the circle. The rest of us were on the tree and whenever he tried to catch one of us, some other boy would jump down, touch the stick and hurl it far. Ranga would then have to run after the stick. What a fall this was from his cricket where he lorded it over everyone! In our game he was at the mercy of a collection of hooligans—Morris, Terence, Sattar, Wahab—all hell-bent on seeing him humbled in the dust. I tried to give him a chance of catching me by sitting in the lower branches of the banyan. But every time, before he could reach me, another boy would come gliding on a hanging root and touch the stick.

I saw Ranga cry that day. This boy who always appeared cheerful, whether in college or at the bus-stand, playing cricket or travelling in a bus, was now crying, not outwardly but within. One look at his face and you heard the silent scream. This, however, only served to boost Morris' and Terence's sadism to a vandalist ferocity. They kept throwing the stick over the compound wall onto the street. During one of his retrieval jumps over the wall, Ranga tripped and fell and hurt himself badly, but his bleeding knee earned him no respite; he was forced to carry on playing.

After this incident, I didn't expect Ranga to speak to me. But he did come home. (Here the gravitational pull of the Pyari Begum–Nagaratnam combined should not be underestimated.) As for this game of monkeys-on-trees, I had had more than my share of hurt and harassment, though what Ranga had to take was nothing compared to what was dealt out to me, I felt sorry for him. He was older than me, more experienced. Which was really why I went readily with him when he asked me to Krishnaswamy's and his brothers' cricket field. At first I sat watching the whole time, and spoke only to Ranga. A few days later, I picked up a ball that came my way and threw it back to the players. One day when it was nearly dark, Ranga called me to the pitch and asked me to bat. After that it didn't take me long to become a part of their team.

The fact that I had rejoined Krishnaswamy and his brothers after a feud stretching over several years brought me special status. Normally I would have been treated on par with Krishnaswamy's younger brother Balu, who was in my class. But now protocol demanded that I be considered Ranga's equal. Even Balu kept away from me.

In the earlier phase of my cricket, during its good old Santanam era, it was possible for me to have illusions of being an expert. Not any more. Here before me were a set of devoted practitioners of the game. They had put in long hours of sustained practice. Krishnaswamy was good both with the ball and the bat. As for Ranga, he had great style, but his batting was poor. Krishnaswamy's brothers, Balu and Goku, were both splendid bowlers, especially Goku. Three balls in every over he bowled came straight to the middle stump.

During my first few days in this group it was invariably Goku who bowled to me. Most often his very first ball would come straight for my wicket. Within the few seconds it took for the flying ball to reach me, I was fairly certain that it wouldn't fail to hit its target. Yet, I would make an effort with my untrained limbs and body to stop it, conscious of a crippling sense of inadequacy, anger, sorrow, despair and anxiety. And then I would wait for the crash which was sure to follow in the next split second when the leather-covered sphere of five and a half ounces struck the metal-capped pieces of wood, and I was seldom disappointed. The loud cheers that followed the fall of other players were not heard when I was bowled, only remarks like 'Bad luck' or 'Better luck next time'. All because I was close to Ranga, and Ranga was the equal of and in certain respects better than Krishnaswamy. My cricket, however bad it was, drew very guarded comments because of my exalted position. But being considered Ranga's equal had its problems as well. It deprived me of the coaching which is the privilege of a young novice. For me the daily drill was: go in to bat—face Goku's ball—get bowled out—hand the bat to the next player and leave. That was all. Ranga's friendship for me, however, was not contingent on my expertise or lack of it in cricket.

Meanwhile, Morris' eldest sister became thinner and thinner. Terence ran away from home and then returned. A big explosion in Bombay harbour claimed a large toll of lives. Many buildings were damaged. A Parsi family in Lancer Barracks claimed that during this explosion, a block of gold descended through the roof of one of their relatives' houses in Bombay. A collection was started by *Kalki* magazine in Madras for a memorial for the poet Bharati at his birthplace Ettayapuram. The contributors' list was published for months on end in this magazine. Two lines recorded the efforts of my father and two others in our city in this cause. Madras and Tiruchi stations began to be received in the evenings on our secondhand GEC radio set, fragmented by crackling static which got worse every day.

In the Regimental Bazaar, a vegetable shop, a grocery and three flower stalls were destroyed. All these stood opposite a small mosque. The police fired three rounds in which a boy was hit below the knee.

Krishnaswamy got an apprentice's job somewhere in the north. He quit his studies and within a week had quit the place as well. Ranga and I became the leaders of our two cricket teams. We had three Telugu boys playing with us now. We harried them outrageously and spoke to them only in Tamil, though whenever they talked about the fear that pervaded Hyderabad and Secunderabad those days, we listened intently.

Goku continued to get me out with his fourth or fifth ball. It was then that a few Muslims began to practise hockey on our playground. They kept directing their white ball towards us. One day Kamesh, a boy in our group, picked it up and threw it away. At this, the whole hockey group converged upon us with raised sticks. They hit Padmanabhan on the head, drew blood and fled from the place. We hoped that as he was a high official, Padmanabhan's father would do something about it, but he didn't. We kept away for the next two days. But when it transpired that the hockey group hadn't turned up for play either, we resumed play. We didn't want to abandon the place when we had spent money preparing a good pitch there. Ranga's bowling was spectacular at the time.

After Krishnaswamy left, our group played a match with a rival team with Ranga as captain and me as vice-captain. The other side was all out for 81 in the match. We played next. Our score was 77 according to their score book, but 102 according to ours. It was Ranga who had written down the score most of the time. The other boys set up a cry of 'Cheating!', 'Cheating!' and asked Ranga to sign. Before I knew what was happening, our team had run away from the field and Ranga with them, leaving me to cope. As vice captain I was forced to sign in the book. I wrote an illegible 'Ramaswamy' instead of my real name. I was out for a duck as usual in that day's match. There had been a Goku in the rival team as well!

One day Ranga announced that he was leaving Secunderabad, and then his family left the place. Ranga never came back.

And I became captain of our cricket team.

3

Chandru pedalled home at full speed. As he approached the Raniganj railway bridge, Narasimha Rao stretched out an arm and stopped him. 'Where are you coming from?' he asked Chandru in a voice taut with anger.

'Cricket practice.'

'Where?'

'At the college.'

Narasimha Rao spat out scornfully. *'Thoo!'*

'Why "thoo"?'

'Aren't you ashamed to play with those halfs?'

There was a time when Chandru didn't know what the 'half' referred to. It was Morris who had enlightened him by making a Muslim boy take down his shorts.

'Well?'

'Nasir Ali Khan is the captain, isn't he?'

'So what?'

'Thoo!'

'Let me move on now,' Chandru said. 'It's dark and I don't have a light on my bicycle. A lot of people are being caught for it these days.'

'Is that surprising?' Narasimha bristled, 'When every single policeman here happens to be a Muslim. It's only we Hindus who are booked for all these things. Invariably. Do any of these bastards, these Razakars, bother about their bicycle lamps and all that? Are they ever caught for it? And think of all those people who roam the streets with swords and knives. Are they rounded up by the police? Never. But here you go blithely playing with these people. The times aren't made for play, can't you see that, you fool? And by the way, do you know, you boot-licker of Nasir Ali Khan, that his father offers military training to the Razakars?'

Chandru was amazed at Narasimha Rao's easy arrogance, the presumption that everyone else was an ignoramus. It was not as if Chandru had been ignorant of the activities of the senior Khan. Why, he'd seen the whole family. He'd never been able to think of Nasir's sister as a mere human. As for the father, there was something extraordinary about his personality too despite his huge moustache, bloodshot eyes and sheer bulk. Nasir, however, had the rare gift of the common touch. Along with his arrogant and commanding manners, he had a graciousness that allowed him to mix easily with humbler people like Chandru. He had had a taste of it today at the nets. What had happened was this.

Nasir had called out 'Next!' but the player at the net continued to bat. After he hit two balls, Nasir bellowed out in English, 'Get out!' Without waiting for any further orders, Chandru walked up to the net and stood before the wicket.

He had never practised cricket like this, surrounded by nets on three sides, like some animal in a cage. A strong rope-net some six foot high had been stretched between the four poles at the corners of a flattened 'U', the opening being meant for the bowlers to bowl from. The net was not tied tight and it flapped continuously, distracting Chandru as if someone was clapping to call his attention. Luckily for him, the first bowler was slow. The ball pitched some ten feet in front of him. He tipped it but the ball went ripping through the air, perhaps because it was hit at a crucial angle. The next ball bore down fast upon him and nearly struck him. He raised his bat in self-defence and hit it. This deflected the ball which soared away but was stopped by the nets which began to sway furiously.

After that, during those alarmingly endless minutes of play, he was unable to block or drive properly. The stumps fell twice and he was also hit by a ball on his thigh.

Any moment now, Chandru was expecting the captain's words, 'Next batsman!' All his illusions about his prowess at cricket lay shattered after the first minute. This game was not for him. A man born to the game would play well under every circumstance and with everyone. Every game is a journey towards a destination, and a good player completes it quickly, confidently, unhesistatingly. But he must also have an intuitive knowledge of the game or should have acquired it through practice so that he plays it with every part of his being, every cell in his body. To watch Nasir play was to realise this intense communion between the player and his game. Whatever had made Chandru get himself so foolishly trapped in the nets today? The three bowlers had almost certainly vowed to themselves to shatter him to smithereens today. Why was it that even the slow bowlers had turned so vicious? Net practice which had appeared so easy from the outside, had turned into a horrid experience. But the flip-flap of the net and the unremitting attack of the balls had not deterred the boy who had played before him. *He* had not been flustered. In fact, he had been eager to continue in the face of the captain's displeasure. He could, poor boy, have been asked to play some more. And where was the need to make me bat anyway, thought Chandru. Having already refused to bowl, there was no way he could refuse to bat when asked. Nasir might easily have rounded on him and asked, 'Why the hell did you come then?'

Here is Sundar Singh bowling again. The friction between him and me is long standing. Something always happens to aggravate it. First, there was this thing about the tickets. I had sold a few tickets for our college play to four of Sundar Singh's neighbours. He seems to have approached some people later with his quota of tickets and found that he couldn't sell any. So he came and shouted at me. Then there was the business of Padma Sivarao. Padma Sivarao was the only reasonably good-looking girl in our science section. The science section as a rule never attracted more than five or six girls. During the practical sessions, each cupboard in the laboratory had to be shared by two students. Sundar Singh and Padma Sivarao were a diad at first, but later she asked for a change of partner. Perhaps she was put off by Sundar Singh's sideburns. She was timid by nature. Possibly it was some defence mechanism at work. Anyway, it was I who was chosen to replace Sundar Singh, though there must have been thirty names between mine and hers in the attendance register. Sundar Singh's chagrin is evident in every ball that he bowls at me, savagely aiming at my head. He keeps it up, intent on denying me a breather. This wretched mat spread on the ground seems to have joined the conspiracy against me. It hasn't been nailed down properly. A big tear on its bumpy surface just where I stood keeps tripping me up. Here comes another ball, from another slow bowler this time. The ball goes up in an arc, curves down and spins off at an angle—an easy one to play on other days—but now it sails past me. My bat is nowhere in its path. This is net practice, it isn't meant to just block the ball without taking any risks, as may happen in a match. Everyone is keen to tackle every ball, however well bowled and difficult. That boy who played before me, what a ferocious hitter he was! And here I stand, trying to block the ball and failing. Here's Sundar Singh again. The rascal, the blackguard. I wonder who chooses these people to bowl. The same person who asked me to bat, I suppose. If Sundar Singh persists in aiming at my head with a full toss every time, his chances for a place in a team are rather slim. Maybe, that's why he is enjoying himself here. Everyone is. I should too if I weren't like a mouse in a trap. Here is another ball coming straight for the wicket. It shouldn't be a problem. Left foot forward, bring the bat down and the ball ought easily to take off for extra cover. Hell, it's gone. I'm clean bowled again. In a real match, one would have been spared this humiliation of continuing to play. Once out, the batsman can leave the field. With nets, one has to set up the wicket oneself and begin to bat again. The ball escapes the bat, hits the net, and then comes the most humiliating part—I pick it up and toss it back. There's no point in playing like this. Am I practising to bat or to pick up the ball? Here comes Nasir himself to bowl. His bowling resembles mine somewhat. If I had trained with good players from the age of five as he had done, and like him, had had no thoughts but cricket on my mind every minute of my life, I could now have been bowling like him, or even better. No, perhaps not. Because even the minutest movements of a good player should be infused with the game. That is what is lacking in me...

Here comes Nasir's ball, pitching far off. Meant to be hit with the body swinging on the well-planted right foot, and a sure boundary at square leg. But no, I swung the bat a bit too early before the ball could reach me, and—splat! What was that hitting my thigh? Nasir said, 'Sorry, dost.' Nothing for him to be sorry about. Sheer incompetence on my part. But then I had captained the team for a whole year, hadn't I? And been quite successful at it. Though it was a mixed team of young and old, and only three could boast of some sort of cricket boots. I myself had played barefoot for four months before I had a pair of boots made for twelve rupees. Cheap, wasn't it? Not much to look at, though. How could one expect anything better from the cobbler under the tree? But the boots were quite comfortable...

This tear in the mat keeps tripping me up. Here comes another ball from Nasir. Must play it well. Thank God I was able to block it, but then I was blocking a ball which ought to have been smashed with a powerful swing. Now it's a shortie bowling, not bowling, just slinging. He wouldn't be allowed to do that in any match. His ball always comes rolling over the ground. Wonder how he manages it. Like Ramanathan in my old team whom we called 'the ground ball roller'. Curses. Another miss. I won't come for net practice in future. Never. But then how does one get into the college team without any net practice? Might have been possible if one had proved oneself beyond doubt and had won recognition outside. Nasir has certainly proved himself. And yet, look at him here today, fielding and bowling like the rest of them. Is it a sign of overconfidence that he hasn't yet come to bat? Or is it just self-restraint—that as the captain he must be careful not to take any undue advantage? He allots the other boys their turns at bowling and batting, often choosing the most unlikely players. Look at this now, a lot of boys got no more than four or five balls, but this Sundar Singh has been at it for hours. It's been hell. How does one escape a ball aimed at one's head in this cramped net? There's room enough to save your head, just. Even great players must have gone through a spell of training in a similar cage. I've watched some of the big names myself here on this very ground, always watched with a welling desire to play myself. That was one reason I put up with that unruly team, with Balu, Kamesh, Goku, Ramanathan, Aleck...

Now this Sundar Singh is bowling exactly like that Venkatesh. They must get their rice from the same grocer. Now this ball here. I drove it to the right, but it went somewhere else. Nasir bowling again. The ball comes sailing through the air humming with its spin as it comes, and pitches exactly six inches in front of me. Ought to have hit it before it touched the ground. Failing that, one could have pushed it off with a forward tilted bat placed just at its pitching point. A dangerous ball this. Should be warded off, sure to get bowled otherwise. Nuisance of it, why is it that my hand foolishly swings the bat? Bowled! Won't this Nasir ever call out 'Next batsman!'. Has he decided to keep me in this cage forever and subject me to every indignity in the game? This is perhaps his way of asking me, more or less, 'How dare you come to play with the likes of us? Playing with a rag-tag team for a year doesn't qualify you for a place in the college team, understand?' Is he humiliating me in public? I shall never play here. Not with these snobs. Never. Never. Never. These lords and nawabs and their games are not for me. Not at all...

'Next batsman!'

Chandru stood gazing at Narasimha Rao's face before him. It was a dark, handsome face with a broad jaw and a high forehead. A fine dignified specimen of a man from Andhra. But God help you if you happened to call him that. He belonged to Andhra all right. But he wished to be called a Telangana man, emphasising the region of Andhra to which he belonged. He came from a Telugu-speaking family that had been in Hyderabad for generations. But they spoke Urdu at home most of the time. He was near-Muslim himself. Yet here he was, accusing Chandru of hobnobbing with Muslims. But then the boy had no means of knowing what Nasir had said to Chandru at the end of the day's practice, 'Why, friend, anything the matter today?' That was all he had said.

'Narasimha, let me go now,' Chandru said. 'I'll see you tomorrow. No lamp on my bicycle, you see.'

Chandru bit his tongue for bringing up the subject of the bicycle lamp again. But Narasimha Rao did not detain him.

Chandru rode through the labyrinth of narrow lanes that connected James Street and Kingsway. The streets were usually so congested that manoeuvering a bike through them called for considerable skill. But there were very few people on the streets now. Not that there had been any riots here. But several long-settled Muslim families had moved down from here to predominantly Muslim localities in Secunderabad. At the same time, several Hindu families had also sent their women and children out of the state. The place was now almost deserted so that Chandru was able to ride without ringing his bell. Those who had moved out of there had been simple folk, petty vendors of vegetables, betelnut or fruit, and hawkers who pushed their food-carts through the streets. They sold very tasty food like vadas and murukus which cost just a rupee a seer. An anna's worth could be quite filling. The same things sold for two annas in the restaurants. They had fled now, all those who made a living filling their hands and stomach for a single anna. The Muslim refugees had now taken over their street-food trade. Let a thousand more like them set up shop here, and the city would gobble it all up and ask for more. Thus it wasn't as if the earlier lot had left for fear of competition. It was something else that had driven them away. This Hindu-Muslim thing had been festering for nearly a year and had finally come to a head on Join Indian Union Day. That day there had been processions, police baton charges and arrests in Hyderabad city. In Secunderabad shops were closed and nobody attended school. Things would have passed off peacefully but for what happened in Regimental Bazaar.

Chandru passed the Islamiah High School. A policeman was sure to be around. He must push the bicycle, not ride it. There was no other way.

Then suddenly, two men sprang on Chandru. 'Who are you?' asked one. 'Bomman,' said the other, as if he were answering the man,

'Kill him!'

All Chandru felt were the first two blows.

4

Chandru fell. His bicycle fell on top of him, luckily as it turned out, for it took most of the beating.

Some people ran across from another alley with shouts of *"Kill!"* Chandru's attackers saw them come and fled with the second group at their heels.

Hardly fifty yards away, Secunderabad's Monda Market hummed with activity. Yet, the lane Chandru was in was deserted. He pulled himself together and stood up.

As he wheeled his bicycle and walked towards Monda he wondered how he had survived that furious swirl of sticks with minimal damage to himself. Perhaps his assailants had not intended to kill him, just to beat him up.

The crowd at Monda seemed thinner than usual. Until a few months ago, every inch of space on the platform or on the floor was covered with vendors' wares. Now the shops had thinned out. The large and impressive platform was now occupied by vendors selling onions, aubergine, chilli, clusterbeans. Those who sat at the foot of the platform sold spinach and greens. A great variety of leaves glimmered in the light of the tin oil lamps with stout wicks which gave out as much smoke as light. The greens had helped them out in the World War years when rice was not to be had and one had to content oneself with maize rotis. Young people managed with any kind of diet but adults had a difficult time with a daily diet of greens. But spinach was practically the only thing available in the market those days. All other vegetables would be scooped away by military contractors.

Their army trucks would line up from eleven in the morning, blocking the way to the market. They never stopped to bargain, just paid the asking price, loaded their trucks with large sacks of vegetables and cleared the stocks in no time. But even in those days when Nagpur aubergines, too large to be held in your palm, were in season, you got two seers for an anna. If you bought in bulk you got forty seers for a rupee, that is eighty pounds a rupee. Sacks full of aubergines would be brought home in large baskets by porters. Then the heap would be chopped and the pieces dried in the sun—the whole process would take weeks—then tightly packed in clay pots and stored. Those aubergines were not to be seen these days, thought Chandru. Few things came to Hyderabad from outside.

It was a different sort of arrival these days. 'Refugees' for one. Must look up the spelling.

Chandru walked in the direction of Monda. The place presented a curious spectacle at this hour when the day had ended and the night had begun. The day's crowds had gone, only a few people lingered about. The vegetable vendors and the women selling greens would also leave soon. They would leave a few things spread on the floor, onion, garlic, dried chilli and grain. In the naked flame of the smoking oil lamps, a few paise worth of goods would change hands. This petty trading would go on until half-past eight. Then they would wind up and go home.

Home? What sort of a home? And where? At night the vendors collected their wares in baskets, covered them with empty baskets and sacking. Some of them went to sleep beside their bundles. It wasn't long before the whole platform at Monda was covered with them. A few had already begun to appear.

As Chandru wheeled his bicycle along, his cricket boots beat sharply on paved floor. The strong granite and cement flooring had given way under the assault of the ceaseless trundling of barrows. Then Chandru's foot caught in a pothole and the boots came up coated with slush.

Chandru was walking at a normal pace. Somehow that attack hadn't shaken him. He hadn't seen the faces of his assailants though they must have seen his. He was sure they were not refugees. If they were they would be huddled in those makeshift shelters on Station Road a furlong away. There were twice as many women among them as men, ranging from old women to little girls. And the children swarmed all over the place. There were too many squeezed into a tiny pocket of this small city. The places they had left behind may not have been much to boast of, but then they *were* places they had been born and grown up in. Even beggars would find an alien city forbidding. Yet this was the fate of not just a few but millions of Indians in the north, caught in the holocaust of the partition. Whole villages had been plundered, women in their hundreds raped and abducted, people hounded out of their homes and hacked down. Those who had fled their homes were not spared either. Refugee convoys, refugee trains, people clinging to the roofs and the carriage-couplings were all fair target for the butchers. Some refugees had walked mile after mile witnessing the slaughter, rape and abduction of their kith and kin. But all these horrendous happenings a thousand miles away had been mere news on the radio here so far, only a blurred image at the edge of one's consciousness. Even the knock Chandru had received was too slight to bring home the total horror of the situation.

He knew that just as the Muslims in their hundreds sought refuge in Hyderabad, Hindu and Sikh refugees had descended on Delhi in their thousands, in their millions. Having lost all to the bestial lust of humans, they were beasts now themselves. But amidst this wilderness of churning, heaving, terror-struck humanity was a figure raising his lone voice in a hymn: 'Ishwara Allah tero naam'. Chandru had never seen him, though. Not yet. Not even once. But then Hyderabad never seemed to have a place in the great man's itinerary.

Three cows accosted Chandru. Whose? Who knew? Scores of stray cattle, mostly cows and calves, had the freedom of Monda. Cattle from other localities were rounded up and impounded by the police. But the cattle of Monda were impervious to all such threats. They visited all the vendors, waited for the moment when their attention would stray, and treated themselves to huge mouthfuls of beans, potato, banana and gourd. Beating and shooing had little effect on them. While a shopkeeper was intent on haggling over a half-anna, he would lose a whole eight annas' worth to these marauders in no time at all. Apparently, the shopkeepers themselves had set aside a share of their merchandise for these cattle who fattened themselves at public expense but whose milk was for others.

Chandru scratched the head of one of the cows before him while still holding on to the bicycle. The cow craned its neck forward to be rubbed. One by one, the other cows began to lean on his bicycle, awaiting their turn for a scratch. Chandru soon found his fingers aching and the nails began to burn. But the cows were in no mood to leave him. Chandru's mind went back to their buffalo at home and the thrashing he had given it earlier that evening. It made him sad to think of it. But then a buffalo could never nuzzle up to one as gracefully as these cows. Everything a buffalo did, from the flapping of its tail to the sudden scampering off at seeing you approach was awkward, ill-timed and ungainly. But the way these cows—never mind whose they were—offered their faces for a caress, one would think they had been snuggling up like that for years.

Chandru pushed his bicycle forward, shouting at the cows: 'Out! Out of my way!' As they reluctantly made way for him, the handle-bar of his bicycle scraped against the stomach of a cow, causing it to shiver. There was an outer fringe of buildings that surrounded Monda like a fortress. It housed a number of wholesale grocery shops, most of them closed now. Many of them were not provided with a light at all, so sure were the merchants that their business would never outlast the sun's light. One shop was, however, still open. It stood apart from the rest, set a little away from the road, an oil store. In the backyard were the oil presses and the oil vendor's house. The shop sold oil wholesale as well as retail. You could buy barrels of oil or just a seer or two. A small boy looked after the till. Chandru asked him, 'Where's your mother?'

'In the house.'

'Could you call her?'

The boy went in. After a while, a fat woman came out. She was from Rajasthan. The patches of oil on her clothes were visible even in the dim light.

She said, 'Don't you see it's past the lighting hour. Why did you come so late?'

'I haven't come for oil. Just to leave my boots here. May I? I'll come for them in the morning.' She didn't understand what Chandru said. So he kicked a booted foot at the ground to explain. Still not sure what was expected of her, she said, 'All right.' Chandru stood his bicycle on the street and climbed the four steep steps that lead to the shops and took off his boots.

Now she asked, 'So the shoe pinches, does it?'

'No, it's just that it's impossible to walk with these on.'

'What brought you to Monda after dark?' she asked. 'Is your father with you?'

'I was delayed at college,' I said.

'You'd better hurry home now. There are plenty of thugs around.'

With that, she suddenly became suspicious. 'Why, were you beaten up by any chance?'

Chandru looked up at her, boots in hand. 'Yes.'

She started to shout, and a young man appeared when he heard the noise. 'Calm down, Mother, calm down,' he said.

The woman gripped Chandru and asked him, 'Where? Where did they hit you?'

'On the back. Just a couple of times. By then some people ran by that way. The men saw them and bolted.'

'But who were these people?'

'Why, the Arya Samajis, of course.' It was the young man who had spoken.

The woman now shifted her attention from Chandru to him, her older son. 'Go in. At once. Get in now.'

'Stop it, Mother,' he said. Then he asked Chandru, 'Where did they attack you?'

'Near the High School.'

'Are they people you know?'

'No.'

The woman screamed at her son. 'Go *in*. Now go!' To Chandru she said, 'Please leave at once. Don't get us into trouble. Go, get away from here.' She began to haul the oil tins into the shop.

Chandru tied his boots together and hung them on his biycle. This was the shop where his father always bought the cooking oil the family needed. Even in those days when the railways had taken it upon themselves to supply them with groundnut oil along with their rationed cereal, they had depended on this shop for their sesame oil. They never needed more than two seers of oil, but Father, fastidious as ever, always bought it from this Rajasthani shop, patiently waiting at the mill for the freshly crushed oil. Chandru and his younger brother who used to sit along with Father on these occasions, used to get a bit of jaggery to eat from this woman. Ever since her husband's death several years before this, she had run the oil mill herself. Her son had now grown old enough to join the Arya Samaj and was receiving training in weilding sticks. Certain people were sure to have their eye on this young man and his shop, though nothing untoward had happened yet.

It was so much easier to walk barefoot. Chandru went on a circuitous route to avoid Station Road which was packed with refugees. The playground of the SPG school with St Thomas' Church at one end seemed to move along with him. He never could figure out how the school attached to this church got its name. Until a few years ago, people used to walk across its grounds, but now there were high walls on all sides and a locked gate.

Manohar Talkies marked the westernmost point of the Regimental Bazaar. The cinema hall was on the first floor of the building. The ground floor was let for shops and houses. A lot of people lived there. A film was playing. Soon it would be the interval and half the audience would get 'out passes' and come out to have a cup of tea, or a betelnut bida or a glass of sweetened buttermilk from Govardhan's shop. The place hadn't changed much. Not yet. The shops wore a drowsy look all day but woke up to work in the evening. Even the whir of the tailors' sewing machines could be heard only during the evening and night. The area round the Manohar Talkies building was full of clumps of people talking. Harigopal was sure to be somewhere here with his friends even now. But then Harigopal's house was near, he could afford to stay out talking till eight-thirty at night. Not everyone was as lucky. Lancer Barracks was still at least a mile away. It wouldn't do to get spotted by Harigopal now.

An unmetalled road branched off ahead, poorly lit. Chandru took the road. Some of the many houses on either side of the street had electric lights, but the majority were lit only with hurricane lanterns. The street itself was neither dark nor deserted. The chatter that filled the air at all hours of the day came from the girls in green skirts and blouses who stayed in the St Francis Convent girls' hostel. Next to it was St Mary's Boarding, an orphanage for boys which housed a school and a hostel in the same compound. Orphans yes, but the boys did not lack for mischief. No boy could be well-behaved when about fifty girls lived within peeping distance just on the other side of the wall. The boys were initiated early into an awareness of the other sex.

This awareness had been with Chandru for some time now. Life had been such a straightforward uncomplicated affair before these stirrings made themselves felt. Chandru was now passing through the Kusini Paracheri slum. He remembered how as a small boy he had taken the name to be pejorative. He later found it was the name used by those who lived there. This slum was the only fully Tamil-speaking locality in this predominantly Telugu city where Urdu was the second important language. But what Tamil! He found their dialect almost unintelligible. All the men here claimed to be butlers serving English people, barring a few who were car drivers. The men were not gregarious. Even when a group sat together over cards, they were never noisy, perhaps because of the customary restraint they had to practise in the English people's houses where they worked. The women compensated amply though for the men's reserve, conducting their quarrels for hours together, screaming at the tops of their voices, ever hovering near a climax but always stopping just short of violence. The men would be present throughout, sitting around smoking bidis, even dozing off. When they woke, if they found the women still belting it out, they redoubled their efforts at yawning. It was a place full of dirt and slime, onion peel and chicken bones, dogs and pigs. The reek of roasting meat and the screams of coarse, ear-polluting invectives filled the air. But even in this slum, there were a few girls whom Chandru noticed. Why, he'd even managed to find out the name of one of them. Pushpa.

He was at Keyes High School now. This short stretch was indeed full of schools. Keyes High School was the biggest and the most prestigious girls' school in Secunderabad. A variety entertainment by the girls with tickets sold to the public was an annual ritual here. Plays, one in Tamil, one in Telugu, some group and solo dances, a few jokes, a brief address by the headmistress followed by an elaborate one by the chief guest—Chandru had seen it all nearly every year since one or the other of his sisters, older or younger, was sure to be a pupil there. The last time he attended this school entertainment, however, he felt self-conscious, something he had never felt before. Nervous, shy, expectant, glad and aroused, he had been in the grip of an unsettling mix of emotions. A change had indeed come over him, making him a little like the boys in the boarding school.

Chandru kicked the ground. For some time he had been aware of these new stirrings that were crowding out the old thoughts. This state of mind was brought on by a woman, but a woman with no individual identity. She was a mere she, female. Any girl he saw on the street merged with this she and set up a tumult in his mind. The list of his women tormentors was by now rather long, from Pyari Begum next door to Pushpa in the Pariah settlement. There was also the brigade of those whose names he didn't know, like Nasir Ali Khan's sister. Now wait. Could it be that he'd gone to cricket practice today for her sake?

Chandru kicked the ground viciously with his unshod foot—not a wise move, especially when you had a bicycle alongside. He bruised his big toe. It began to bleed. Ah! That was some relief. The sight of blood, he found, was soothing to one's mind. This cruel streak was a recent development. The wild thrashing he had given the buffalo that evening had been part of this compulsion. It was only now, after all these hours that Chandru realised how cruel he had been to the animal. He felt it all the more due to the blows he had himself received. Well, unlike that absolutist Narasimha Rao, Chandru had never found it easy to make moral judgements, to have clear distinctions between good and evil. That confrontation with Narasimha had indeed given him a severe jolt, but he hadn't become fully alive to the situation in the city till the woman at the oil mill had driven him out. 'Don't get us into trouble. Go, go away from here.'

The woman had not really wanted to drive him away though. It was just that even Monda, though apparently safe, was far from that. The times were such that all over the country, under a sudden diabolical spell, unbelievable things had been happening to unlikely people in unexpected places, places that had known no strife for years, places much safer than our Monda. But at such a time, just look at me, wheeling my bicycle along this dark alley, hoping for a glimpse of Pushpa, dreaming of a girl from a royal family whose name I don't know, and going to cricket practice conducted by her brother.

No. No. No. No. Chandru kicked the ground again and pummelled the handlebar of his bicycle. This time his feet were certainly injured, which meant that he wouldn't be able to put on his cricket boots till the bruises healed, which in turn meant that even if Nasir chose to ask him again to cricket practice, he wouldn't be able to go. Ah, respite at last. Respite from all the ugly thoughts that were churning up his psyche.

Even after entering the Lancer Barracks compound, Chandru continued to wheel his bicycle rather than ride it, though there was no need for this. It was just that he felt disinclined to change his mode of locomotion for the last few yards after having used it for a whole two miles. Lights were on in all the houses. Numbers twelve, eleven, ten, nine—Janardhan in his underwear—back to the door—eight, seven, the Mannas' house—Morris, Terence, Julie, Laura. Julie would be sitting staring at a corner. Laura, lying supine on the floor, listening to a gramophone in very bad repair, playing a record in very bad shape. Mrs Mannas would be asleep. Mr Mannas would be drinking. The radio was blaring out a typically Islamic song broadcast from Hyderabad Radio. Listeners' Requests would go on the air in half an hour. But of course there was no chance of listening to these Hindi songs in his house. His family tuned in only to the far-off Tamil stations, Madras or Trichy, no matter how bad the reception.

Father didn't seem to have returned. Mother was waiting in the veranda. 'Why are you late?' she asked.

'Got delayed.' What an answer, thought Chandru even as he said the words.

'But I asked you why.'

Chandru stood his bicycle against the wall and went straight in to the back of the house, climbed down the steps and walked up to the buffalo shed. The buffalo saw him in the dark and shuffled about to register recognition as it were. Restless circling of the stake had shortened her tether considerably. Chandru unwound the coils and refastened the rope allowing it a fair length. Then he put an arm round the buffalo's neck and hugged her, and was rewarded with a flick of its dung-coated tail.

When he came into the house again and the bright light shone on his face, Mother noticed it at once. 'What's that big lump you have on your forehead, son?' she asked.

'Oh that. I was hurt playing cricket.'

5

I was all this time under the impression that Father had lost his money in the Arbuthnot Bank. But it seems to have been the Quilon Bank, not Arbuthnot. The man who lost in the Arbuthnot collapse was my grandfather. It had all happened long before the collapse of the Quilon Bank. How much would my grandfather have lost? Some eighty rupees, perhaps. Anyway, losing money in the bank seems to have been a hereditary hazard in our family.

The man who got the blame for the collapse of the Quilon Bank was Sir C.P. Ramaswamy Iyer. But this is all mere hearsay heard from other sources, none of them reliable; from people who couldn't remember in the morning where they had left their snuff boxes at night.

As for this Sir CP, I have seen a few photographs of him always in profile, turban round his head. These photographs used to put me in mind of those turbanned heads drawn on the walls of certain sheds set apart in railway stations. The logo was completed by a word written beneath the figure: 'GENTLEMEN'. There would be another profile at the other end of the shed, of a woman, with the word 'LADIES'.

Perhaps in those days Sir CP's face was considered ideally suited for all graphic representations of manhood.

Father never stepped out except in that uniform favoured by Tamil migrants, his shirt tucked into a dhoti and a coat over the shirt. The dhoti was worn with an end of the cloth separating the legs. We called it the bicycling dhoti. If he wore a cap it meant he was going to the office. No headgear was used for other trips. I had made countless trips to these other places with my father ever since I learnt to walk. And after we came to Lancer Barracks, buying any little thing involved a two-mile trek to the market.

Father would start on one of his little expeditions in order to fetch some vegetables or a little mustard. He wore red ear-studs, the stones dimmed with grime. His hair was gathered into a knot. I would go and stand before him in my oversized shorts and double-breasted coat. This coat, made when I was in my third or fourth standard, served me till I entered the ninth since it was sewn to fit a growing boy. It wasn't that I liked the coat. But going out with father wasn't possible without it. When we were barely ten paces from home, Father would stop and enquire of Jaffar Ali, 'How are you, master?' Mr Jaffar Ali would be watering his beloved crotons, a large pipe in his mouth. These friendly chats stopped when we acquired buffaloes and it became known that they had a predilection for crotons. The half-hour chat with Mr Jaffar Ali ended when Mr Mannas would peep out of his house, which was next. A 'What mister?' from Father signalled the next half-hour's chat—with Mr Mannas this time. At other times I would have gone straight in and helped Mrs Mannas who would be peeling onions to the accompaniment of muttered imprecations. But when with Father, I just stood at the gate, observing him and Mr Mannas minutely while between them the English language was hanged, drawn and quartered. If the older Mannas girls happened to pass by, I wouldn't even acknowledge their presence. A few yards further, Father would stop to talk to Mr Kesava Rao, greeting him with the Telugu version of 'What mister?', 'Emi babu?'. Half an hour later, Father would be at Mr Masilamani's, buttonholing him with the Tamil version of 'What mister?', 'Enna dorai?' Fifteen more minutes were lost in this way. Father never took the wider roads on these trips to the market. It was always through the lanes and bylanes, turns and about-turns. Rarely did we pass an alley without his stopping to point out a house with remarks like, 'This is where we were when the plague struck.' Or 'This was our home during the floods.' Any old woman glimpsed on these premises would prompt a half-hour chat. I wondered if it was to indulge his nostalgia that Father chose this route through the lanes visiting his erstwhile habitations. If the pride of the Mohenjodaro civilisation was its underground drainage system, one could say this of Secunderabad that its culture resided in its maze of lanes and alleys.

Many of these lanes had waist-high stone poles erected at their entrance to prevent the entry of vehicles. But even without this precaution, vehicles would never have entered most of these lanes, criss-crossed as they were with open drains and the occasional steps that were needed to connect different stretches of the road which were not all of the same level. There were very few lanes where it was possible for a bullock cart or a tonga to go. The tonga of our town was a horse-drawn coach. What was special about the tonga was that, unlike in the bullock cart, all the passengers could sit with their legs hanging, assuming of course that the number of passengers matched the number prescribed on the tongas themselves. But one never engaged a tonga unless there were at least six passengers. Two in the back seat and two in front were normally accommodated while two more were squeezed in the interstices. This last was the position invariably reserved for me whenever a tonga was engaged by our family.

The process of engaging a tonga was a nuisance. Tongas could be fetched either from the railway station if you walked more than a mile, or from Manohar Talkies, after a convoluted journey through the lanes in quite a different direction. Whatever the route, fetching a tonga was not an adult's job. Nor was it possible to send little boys because they were not likely to be taken seriously by the tongawalas. Thus the task always fell to me. I would mutter my protest before I started on my errand. On the way I would hear Morris' Tarzan-cry as he swung among the roots of the banyan tree. Years later when we left Lancer Barracks, left so many people and things behind, the deepest wrench for me was parting from the banyan. It was here that I played many miserable games of monkeys-on-trees with Anglo-Indian and Muslim boys, with them always throwing the stick over the wall, and me jumping over it to get to the street to retrieve it. Morris and the banyan tree were the two things that never failed to fascinate me. Each time I went to fetch a tonga, it was only after a quick climb up and down a hanging root that I would move on. This of course usually left Morris and my other Lancer Barracks companions speculating on the nature of my errand. What could be more urgent than play?

A call from Lancer Barracks was the last thing likely to whip up any enthusiasm in the tongawalas at the tonga stand. Most times they didn't bother to reply. Someone would, at last, bestir himself to ask where to and how much. I would then ask him in my broken Urdu: what did he expect? Whatever it was, I would agree to it and bring him home. Once back home, I would rush in to look for a safe place to hide. Mother or Father would now ask the tongawala what the fare was. If he said eight annas, they would offer him two annas. The tongawala would then demand to see the boy who brought him there. My people would raise their offer to two and a half annas. He would again ask for the boy. Hot negotiation would follow, after which the man would agree to three annas. Or, equally likely, he would go away in a huff spewing abuse at everyone in the house, particularly me. My father and mother would then accuse me of fixing the fare myself. If only they could have known the travails of a tonga-fetcher, but of course they didn't.

Now for the purpose behind this fetching of a tonga from a mile away. It was to take us all to a Tamil film showing at the tent cinema on the Karbala Maidan three miles away. In the regular cinemas of Secunderabad, Tamil films were shown only once or twice a year, and that for just a week, though Telugu pictures had a run of four to six months and Hindi and Urdu pictures, which came after a showing in Hyderabad city first, ran strong for a couple of months. The Tamil films that lasted two weeks as far as I can remember were just two: *Mangamma Sabatham* and *Sri Valli*. Vasundhara played the role of Mangamma, the woman who takes on a philanderer, and in the mythological film *Sri Valli*, it was Kumari Rukmani, a young girl then, who played Valli. Exhaustive discussions on the charms of these two heroines were held even among elderly people who had shed their inhibitions for the nonce.

The tent cinema showed only Tamil pictures. It was difficult to say what induced the owners to pitch camp in Secunderabad. They showed nearly sixty films in six months. Twenty free tickets would be offered for every two tickets sold. Although a government appointment had become some sort of *memento mori* of modern times, those in authority and their families were always offered special privileges in the tents. The shows would allow a half-hour's late start for them. The first showing lasted until ten o'clock at night and the second started at ten-forty. The footage of films would be cut from 20,000 to 18,000 feet to fit the time available. Whether it was the first or the second show that we went to, the tonga was engaged only to get to the cinema. We always returned on foot in procession for three and a half miles through the streets of Secunderabad at dead of night, rousing the suspicions of at least thirty dogs and disturbing the sleep of several neighbourhoods.

It was quite a common occurrence for a film to be cut in the middle. One day, the film seemed about to break, then it began to run upside down and then quite suddenly it caught fire. We stampeded out of the tent. The show was re-started after half an hour and we went in again. This time we sat in the next class and watched the bit of the film that had survived unburnt. It was Salem Modern Theatre's *Subhadra,* on which a million rupees had been spent, according to the advertisements. The length of the film had already been curtailed by a Government order during the war. The version we got to see was further curtailed by the fire.

Thinking back after all these years of our curious treks back home in the middle of the night, it seems amazing that nothing untoward ever happened to any of us. We took no precautions, had no security measures. My older sister, a fast walker, usually went far ahead of all us. Father and I would be a furlong behind her. Another furlong separated us from my brother and the rest of the sisters. My mother usually brought up the rear all by herself, lagging nearly half a mile behind everyone. On a straight road, we would at least have been within viewing distance of one another. But there were no streets in Secunderabad that ran straight for more than fifty yards. All this, notwithstanding the efforts of a British Resident to build a highway straight as a taut string, to be called Kingsway. When Kingsway finally took shape, however, there were eleven curves within its mile and a half span. What had happened was this: the owners of those houses on the path who would have been affected by the straightening up of the road had out-manoeuvred the British Resident. Every curve was rumoured to have fetched Rs 10,000. Ten thousand rupees was a large sum those days.

Whenever our family procession entered these curves or the so-called short cuts through the bylanes, we lost sight of each other. Victims of a fond illusion that we'd reach home earlier by this route, we would zigzag through the crooked lanes. When we entered a new lane I would grumble to Father, 'This lane is too long, Appa.'

'Let's ask for it to be cut then,' Father would reply.

At the next lane I'd complain again. 'This one is also far too long.'

'Let's cut this as well, then.'

And so we went along, planning to cut lane after lane. When we were not engaged in this discussion of reducing the length of the lanes of Secunderabad, Father would ask me 'Don't these people have a grain of sense? Do they have any brains at all, I wonder.' The reference was to my sisters and Mother for not keeping pace. I never troubled myself for a reply because my ideas concerning the brain and the mind were rather vague. Moreover, Father's tone left no doubt that the questions were merely rhetorical. We traversed the streets of Secunderabad in this curious fashion even when, years later, the city was in the grip of the Razakar terror. For that matter, as close as two days before I was attacked in the street, we had been walking through the streets at night. This time it was a Telugu film, *Gollabama,* not a Tamil one, and Anjali Devi had made her debut in the film.

With her acting and her dancing, this actress zipped her way through the Telugu country and went on to conquer the Tamil country as well. *Gollabama* played more than six months at the Paramount, a permanent cinema theatre. We hardly ever bought tickets. More likely, you'd find our family waiting in a space near the cinema while Father spoke to the manager. We didn't always know this. After half an hour or so, when the manager had been softened up sufficiently, he would come out of his room and ask us to sit in one of the upper stalls. On several occasions, when there were no seats available, extra chairs were brought for us on the manager's orders. We never did see any film from the start, though. Father's habit of persevering for a free pass on every possible occasion was probably an offshoot of his job in the railways. We didn't ever buy tickets for any railway journey either. If it became unavoidable we would have recourse to a PTO which enabled us to pay a third of the usual fare. We undertook a journey of several thousand miles every year just to avail ourselves of this concession.

Our pass would have the names of the starting point and the destination. A column one inch long was provided for entering the names of all the stations we wanted to touch. We were permitted to break journey at these stations. Since this column was too small to include all the places we wanted to visit, the names overflowed, swarming into the margins, left and right, up and down on my father's pass. By the time we returned after we had visited a score of places in two months, we'd be tired of the whole thing. Only once during such a trip was our house burgled, as far as I can remember. But it was our buffalo which presented a nearly unsolvable problem every time. The question of where to leave our buffalo would come up about a month before our journey. People in the milk trade were not likely caretakers as they might not feed the animal properly. A cow of ours had once been starved to death by a milkman. Then there were those who had cattle at home for their own use. But they were not prepared to put up with the additional responsibility of another animal and refused to entertain our requests. The only course we had was to leave the animal with someone in the villages beyond the city, paying him for his services. The problem was that the person might show up a week before we left on our trip—or he might never turn up at all until just before we left. Once we even missed our train because of the buffalo. After that we—Father and I—started to take the buffalo ourselves to Ghatkesar, a village several miles away. Father would take his walking stick along and I would carry an umbrella and a stick. Father wouldn't miss his customary enquiries. 'What babu?', 'What dorai?' and 'What master?' and the buffalo would lead us up and down and roundabout and half the day would be done before we finally reached a village of some ten palm-thatched huts. There we would search for our Mallayya or Sayana, and entrust our animal to him. We would return home by train. Free passes, of course.

The railway pass which was recognised by the cinemas went absolutely unheeded by the customs employees. Our tonga filled with half a dozen people and an equal number of boxes would stop in front of the customs checkpost, an old building situated just outside the Secunderabad railway station. After months of touring far and wide, we had to wait there in a final ten minutes of utter panic. The customs inspector there was a woman, even in those days when the Nizam's territories were supposed to have been in the Middle Ages. It was she who ransacked our boxes and baskets year after year at the end of our trips outside the State. She would go on fishing things out one after the other, while we would go on insisting that everything was brought within the Nizam's territories. The woman, who bore a slight resemblance to Janab Jinnah's sister Fatima, would eye us all very suspiciously and mutter something before she finally took a bunch of hill bananas or a few mangoes for herself and said to us, 'You may go.' I didn't ever see anyone paying customs duty there. She stayed in her job, a permanent fixture like the sun and the moon and the mornings and evenings, ransacking travellers' possessions and dampening the zeal of vegetarians and fruit-eaters even after India's Independence was declared. She was there right through the year-long confrontation of the Government and then for a few months even after the annexation of Hyderabad State by the Indian troops.

My father's usual ebullience got considerably subdued in places like this customs counter and such other precincts which were under the sole jurisdiction of the Nizam's government. No language except Urdu could be used for any transaction in these offices. It would be presumptuous to expect any official to be at his seat at the appointed time. The Nizam's bureaucracy described itself as the Mughalai Durbar. The Mughal Emperor's courtiers posed several possible connotations, the chief one being that nothing happened according to schedule. Eighty per cent of the State Government employees were Muslims; the rest were mulkis, that is, those recognised as natives of Hyderabad State. In those days the Nizam's State Railways offered unmatched opportunities for employment for Tamil persons and others from outside the state. Railway employees always looked down on the minions of the State Government, but living in the State, it was not possible for them to avoid the State offices entirely. On such unavoidable occasions, you found railway employees going in search of Urdu scribes to fill up their forms, and then buying and pasting on the Nizam's court stamps (on which even the numbers were printed in Urdu). You'd find them at the local office at exactly eleven o'clock for the eleven o'clock appointment, waiting there until two, and returning defeated at the end of it all, because neither they nor the local staff had the faintest idea what the other party was talking about. The railway staff were generally treated like an alien horde of plunderers. Father must inevitably have had his share of unpleasant encounters in the corridors of the Nizam's State offices. But then remember my Father's predilection for accosting everyone with the introduction: 'I am a railway servant.' Even if he were to meet a full-throated lion somewhere, this formula I'm afraid, would remain the same. Was it any wonder then that the Mughal courtiers of Hyderabad were not exactly friendly with him?

6 |

There was a large crowd at the Dreamland Cinema. What had been an orderly queue at first turned in a crowd converging on the ticket counter the moment it was opened. If only Morris had been here! He would elbow his way through the crowd till he reached the counter and would then hoist himself upon a few shoulders and get a ticket. Chandru entered the hall without a ticket and curiously, no one stopped him. He was the lone spectator in the hall. A special show of *Bathing Beauty* began for him. The five-foot-nine Esther Williams swam about in the water for a long time before she left the screen. Then she came and stood 'fully clothed now' before Chandru. Two of her upper teeth were a little too big but this only conferred a distinction upon her. She was asking him something sweetly, gently.

'I didn't understand...' Chandru replied.

'Do you like me?' she asked, very clearly this time. Unable to think up a quick answer in English, Chandru was silent. She took him by the hand, led him up to the screen and stepped into the swimming pool with him. Chandru began to tremble.

He was still trembling when he sat up in bed, quite awake. He felt not only ashamed but also afraid. These absurd dreams were a recent development. Was there no way to be rid of them? But there was no one he could turn to for advice.

He got up. The inside of the house was in shadowy gloom. The presence of a roof overhead could only be deduced by the absence of stars.

Chandru came up to the front door. Tall doorways in keeping with the enormous height of the house. The bolt at the top must have been two feet long. Unfastening it was not easy. Special efforts were required. But he had to get out into the open. Had to.

The dim moonlight that filtered through scattered clouds showed things on the ground in silhouette, emphasising the contours. A light mist hung in the air. Lancer Barracks and its environs slept deeply. The strains of a distant song could be heard—a Muslim song with an unmistakably Muslim cadence. A gramophone in some Muslim restaurant would be belting out Zohra Begum or Amirbai Karnataki.

Chandru felt several parts of his body ache—his thigh, hit by the cricket ball at those four square inches unprotected by the pad; his shoulders which had borne the brunt of the Razakars' attack. Were they really Razakars? Actually, it could have been far worse since they had struck from such close quarters. Then there was the diffuse pain in his legs, the result of cycling fifteen miles against the wind in less than four hours and wheeling the cycle along the last three miles because he didn't have a lamp for his vehicle. Those twelve-rupee cricket boots, the handiwork of the cobbler under the tree, weren't good for anything but cricket. The half-mile walk dragging the dead weight of those boots was enough to make your feet ache. Today's walk had been considerably longer. But what was this pain in his side? The buffalo seemed to have butted him.

There was some comfort in the distraction that physical pain offered from the tangles and confusions of the mind. Chandru rubbed his thigh. But though his whole body ached, the pain was not intense enough to drive everything else from his mind.The embarrassment of the dream returned... Nasir Ali Khan. The old man at the bicycle stand. The wind on his face on the Tank Bund. Narasimha Rao. Refugees cooking on the pavement of the road. The fat woman at the police officer's house, the bluish green tracery of veins on her neck and hands... He stood for a while in the open. The shadowy shapes round him took on a more distinct identity as his eyes got used to the dim light. There was a peepal tree in front, with the compound wall of the barracks behind it, and the street beyond the wall. On the other side stood his house, attached to many others in a row. A stretch of open ground, then the banyan tree with its multiple hanging roots. Again the compound wall on that side separating the barracks from the surrounding streets. The street. The street lights. A few bungalows here and there. Strains of music at a distance. A distinctly Muslim tune. The song, a song he had heard so many times over Kasim's radio next door. Pyari Begum was probably asleep now.

Pyari Begum posed a problem. His perception of her had changed recently. She had been no more than a fat girl before. But now, she was not just fat but pretty and deserved a second look. She now looked straight at him as at an acquaintance and did not avert her face.

For some time now, two other families had come to stay with Pyari Begum's family next door. They hadn't come there on holiday. Chandru knew they had come from Sholapur. If Kasim hadn't offered them refuge, they would have been housed in the bamboo shacks on Station Road. They were all Muslims. So was Nasir. But how vastly different they were!

Chandru felt a twinge of regret now. He had not taken proper leave of Nasir Ali Khan. Nasir couldn't be expected to invite Chandru to cricket practice every time. But after the fiasco of that evening, Chandru doubted if he would ever feel like going to the nets again on his own.

Chandru wanted to cry but he couldn't. It had been like this for quite some time now. Laughing heartily, crying openly, expressing one's thoughts freely, all these had become impossible. Months had gone by since he last spoke to Morris and Terence, his neighbours and long-time friends. As for his new friends, he was at a loss to continue any conversation beyond the first two minutes.

Chandru bolted the front door of his house from the outside. He shut the gate and walked towards the peepal tree. Dry twigs from the tree snapped under his feet. He had often collected these twigs and bundled them for the family priest to use to light the ritual fires. The priest had brought a new astrologer home one day. Unlike the general run of astrologers, this one had predicted no glorious future for him. For that matter, this astrologer had never read any of their horoscopes at home without a preliminary pout and a tch-tch. Mother had nicknamed him Saturn, Sani is thought to be dark-complexioned. This astrologer certainly was. He was so dark that it would have been difficult to see him at night. Chandru was thought to be under the sinister influence of Sani right now. His wild speculations next turned to the name 'seven-and-a-half-years' Sani'. Folk etymology made it sound like 'seven-and-a-half-countries Sani'. Did the sinister planet dog your steps through seven and a half countries as well, he wondered. Was he perhaps accompanying him at this moment? Where was he?

Chandru looked around. The block of houses lay stretched like the sleeping giant Kumbhakarna of the *Ramayana*. The second block of the barracks was hidden from view. The spire of the church rose straight into the sky. He had been to the church only that evening, looking for the buffalo. Rough, open country to his right with a few buildings in the distance, and then the Christian cemetery. English ghosts, a hundred years old, would be enjoying themselves here at this hour of night. The place was scary even in the day. But wait, how was it that he could see the cemetery which was half a mile away? Was it perhaps because Saturn was with him?

Then there was the banyan tree. One needed the intervening distance to get a full view of the tree. It looked so incredibly large, as large as a hill. The tiny red fruit on the tree were not visible now. Did they burst after they turned red? Or did they redden and burst after the crows had scattered them to the ground? It didn't matter. The tree was now a dark mass, a charcoal drawing on an immense grey canvas. Not a leaf stirred. But in its own way, it was breathing. In deep silence. Probably oxygenating.

What was that noise? A rustle? A snake. He watched fascinated as it slithered quickly past him. Its path wasn't wavy at all. He stood watching until it merged into the dark and at last was lost to sight. A snake. He had been seeing snakes recently, in fact ever since he had had these dreams. He had seen three during the last few months though he hadn't seen any before that in the nearly eight years he had been in this place. Snakes—the cobra—Nagaratnam. Her name meant the jewel on the cobra.

Nagaratnam. Another girl who one could not pass without turning to look again, a look that never failed to churn up his system. He shouldn't have these thoughts about people who were older, should he? But then did age count in these matters? Besides, of all the girls who interested him, it was Nagaratnam who seemed to reciprocate his interest somewhat—though you never knew for sure—with that twinkle in her eyes. Was it perhaps a Get-away-you-gawky-adolescent sort of look that she gave him?

Chandru had heard things about her from here and there. But only Ranga had given him anything like a cogent account of her. It wasn't inspired by his dislike of her. Nagaratnam had never encouraged Ranga. Maybe there were no specific reasons for her behaviour; maybe there were.

Maybe Ranga's tactics to draw her attention were to blame. But then, boys had been much worse. Ranga was infatuated with her just as half of Secunderabad was. Nagaratnam had become an obsessive topic of discussion with him, but he never got to know her personally. Only those really close to you could ever think it was all right. Others would only talk. Ranga must have ruminated on all the gossip he had heard about Nagaratnam and then come to his own conclusions. But where was Ranga now? He'd left without an address. Couldn't he have written at least a line from wherever he was?

Weighed down by a sense of loss, Chandru wondered if Ranga had befriended him only because of Nagaratnam. No. There had been much more to their friendship than that. Oh for the days they had spent together, walking endlessly and sharing their thoughts.

It was Ranga who had properly initiated Chandru into cricket. But, curiously, as long as Ranga was there, Chandru had learnt nothing. As a batsman, he didn't last beyond the first four balls, and as a bowler, he always found the ball displaying a will of its own. The worst bit was that he wasn't even a good fielder. But a strange thing happened once Ranga left the place. All the techniques that Ranga had taught him so lovingly and painstakingly, all that which eluded him as long as his mentor was present, were now within grasp, just so simple. The ball as it came sailing towards him was no longer a blur. It was now possible for him to talk to the ball, rebuke it and dismiss it from his presence. Even Krishnaswamy's brother Goku of Second

Line Barracks, who used to smirk every time he went to bat, now nursed a feeling of inferiority. When Chandru was chosen captain there had been no murmur of dissent. Even if a few had demurred, and you had asked them to suggest a better name, the answer would have been long coming. In the last three months, Chandru had led his team in seven matches, winning five and drawing two. He had notched up a grand total of 318. Only once had he scored below 30. It was always a 40, 50, even a 77 once. If only Ranga had been there to see him now!

Ranga would then be the captain, of course, but to score like this under him would have been glorious. Ranga's family was among the first to leave Secunderabad because of the Razakar menace. Or was it just that his father had been transferred? Whatever it was, Ranga had left.

The Muslim song had ended. There was a stillness everywhere, not broken even by the hum of crickets. Standing where he was, Chandru turned and looked in all directions. The whole place seemed to have grown. When he looked at his house, it seemed to have moved out quite far. Yet, when he looked at the whole scene with a wide-angled view, the distances were still proportionate, everything was in its place. The world had somehow ceased to be solid—from beneath his feet, it kept flowing, flowing out on all sides, like a picture drawn on the surface of an enormous balloon growing or shrinking as the balloon grew or shrank. As if a hurricane were blowing against a giant bubble in space, making it bulge, squeeze and shake. He himself had grown and grown till he could reach the skies. He could stretch out a hand and pluck a few stars. Then, slowly, the vision began to dissolve back to normalcy, even as he stood pleading with all his heart, 'Oh, no, no. I want it to stay!' Everything became mundane once more—the same old church and the same old cemetery. It reminded him of a painting of an English landscape. A landscape seemed to call for a vista with a few scattered buildings, fields, a stream, some distant hills. A dog or a cow could be allowed somewhere in the painting, but a man never. If he were to be included in the painting of Lancer Barracks, it would cease to be scenic, thought Chandru.

He started to walk towards the banyan tree. At home, he usually avoided the dark recesses, even when there were people around. But now, at dead of night in the open, he felt no fear, or to be more precise, something greater than fear urged him on. But what was he afraid of? Of losing his life? But, unless one knew what life was, was it really possible to be afraid of losing it? Still, it couldn't be denied that he had felt fear, not for any silly reason, but for weighty, sound, substantial reasons. There was some connection between this fear and the other development, this excruciating response to the presence of women. Something seemed to have entered his body—another life, a spirit, a vaporous thing or may be it was just plain water! This thing inside him scared him, it induced dreams. And now, at midnight, it was propelling him towards the tree. He did not really care for the peepal tree. But the banyan tree was a repository of deep memories for him, redolent with countless hours of absorbing play. The banyan tree was like a home away from home. Sitting on its branches he had watched time pass by. Unlike at home, where no relationships were possible unless you bruised yourself with constant activity. You just couldn't hope to escape talking to others. This gentle undemanding tree laid on no such conditions. But then, look at it this way—would it care if I were to be ruined, damned, destroyed? Not at all. So it had its limitations.

Suddenly he felt the moving cinema of his mind cease. He saw a figure under the banyan tree.

Someone was kneeling on the ground, hands covering the face. Was it all right for him to go near? Chandru stood still.

The next minute he knew. He began to walk towards the figure. The woman gave him no indication that she had seen him. Chandru walked up to her as quietly as possible.

'Julie,' he whispered. She gave a start. But she recognised him immediately. 'Chandru! What you doing here man?' she said sniffing. He had been wrong. It was not Julie but Mannas' second daughter Laura. This was all the more surprising because Laura was not the sort of person to sit alone and cry. Though he now felt as close to her as to Julie, he could have sworn that she wasn't the languishing sort. Yet here she was, crying just like her elder sister. Even physically she reminded him of her sister.

'What's the matter?' he asked.

'Oh, nothing. Nothing.' She had controlled herself by now.

'Is there anything I can do? Tell me.'

'Oh, just don't tell anyone you saw me here, like this.'

Chandru hesitated. 'Is anyone else here?'

Laura shook her head. Then she stood up and began to walk towards her house. Chandru called her softly and took her hand in his. She turned back to look at him, still standing where she was. In the dark shade under the banyan, they could not see each other's faces clearly.

Laura said 'Chandru,' then threw her arms round him and began to sob. Chandru held her and stroked her back soothingly. He had been in a similar situation before, with Laura's elder sister Julie. But he had then known the cause of her grief. The soldier who had promised to marry her had vanished without a word. But long after he left, she had clung to the fond hope that he would still return and propose marriage to her. When realisation finally dawned that hers was a hopeless case, she had broken down. But she was a mature woman. Not a mere girl like Laura. Could it be that Laura too had got herself entagled in some such thing, young as she was? He had not seen Laura think of herself as a woman or behave like one until now, when she was crying at midnight, all alone, under the banyan tree.

Laura stopped crying and looked up at Chandru's face. Her eyes glistened in the gloom but their expression could not be read. Chandru wiped her cheeks at a guess. Yes, they were wet.

Laura stood gazing at him for a while. Then she freed herself and walked away. As he watched her enter her house, Chandru smoothed his shirt. Laura had left the scent of some cheap face powder on him.

With Laura gone, Chandru didn't relish the idea of standing alone under the banyan. For the first time that night he felt afraid. The residents of Lancer Barracks led a secluded existence, cut off from the real world beyond. Which was why the two of them had come to a banyan tree on a sleepless night—he, haunted by his cricket memories and she, perhaps, by memories of a lover who had left her. Surprising how they had both come there at the same time. Anyone who had chanced to see them together or happened to hear of their meeting would imagine all sorts of things. Yes, that was just like Lancer Barracks. But in the town outside, there would be many who would be asleep, but also many who couldn't sleep because they were afraid. Fear stalked the city, fast depleting it of its women and children. They were being sent to places outside Hyderabad State. If they began planning such a move in Chandru's family, who would they send and where? And those left behind, was it all right if the Razakars beat them up to a pulp? How long would the Razakars hold the city in terror? And those refugees from Nagpur, were they to make the pavements of Secunderabad their permanent home?

For the first time since he woke that night, Chandru felt his mind return to near normalcy. With increasing clarity came the realisation that no slick solutions were available for any of the questions that troubled him. If only some men would show up now and knock his head in with their staves. His eyes drooped, heavy with sleep.

II

1

It had rained at night the past few days. You wouldn't know it had rained till you got up in the morning. That was how it always rained in this place—a fugitive drizzle now and then. Chandru knew it had rained that night when he put on his shoes in the morning. Only yesterday he had made a resolution never to leave his shoes and slippers on the veranda near the trellis. He could at least have moved them to a safer place before going to bed, but didn't, and now they were soggy and heavy.

Chandru put on his shoes before getting into his trousers. All of them in the barracks—Kasim, Venkat Rao, Jaffar Ali, Mannas, in short, everyone, who wore trousers—did this. By following this sequence, you could avoid crumpling your trousers while bending down to lace up your shoes. Despite these measures, and no matter how carefully you wore the clips at the end of the trousers, a half hour's pedalling was sure to have the trousers ballooning at the knees. It was impossible to get rid of this baggy knee. The creases of your trousers would drop straight till the knee and then follow a curve before they became straight again in the nether regions. But today he wasn't going to ride his bicycle. Three times in the past week he had some trouble or other with his bicycle and Father and Mother both felt it would be better not to take it out till things had calmed down a little. Yes, he'd better not.

Chandru gathered up his books and started for college. A hot sun beat down. Good, his shoes would dry on their own.

The fronts of the houses were all empty, all twelve of them deserted. But this was a mirage-like phenomenon. All of a sudden, the place would fill up with school-goers and office people and those who came out to see them off. Once that happened, it would be impossible to walk past in peace.

You'd have to smile at everyone, stammer out answers to any questions that might be asked and then for all your trouble, finally leave with a bad taste in your mouth. In fact, when Chandru crossed the block he felt nervous. The Mannas house was quite noisy with Terence and his mother shouting at each other. God, there was Laura as well.

Attempting a frozen expression on his face, Chandru hurried on. It was only after he had reached the main road without any further mishap that he felt secure in the anonymity offered by its width and walked towards the station to board the bus for college.

The Secunderabad railway station looked like a granite fortress and the people who moved about in front of the building looked like clockwork toys. The station had a large front and few entry points. An Albion bus decorated with a tin plate marked '7' stood shuddering with its engine on. Once started in the morning, this engine was probably not switched off until the night. Diesel fumes permeated the surroundings. Chandru went round to the entrance of the bus and found that it was full.

A few people waited outside, ready to climb in, when the bus started. He looked inside and felt his spirits sink just a little—Nagaratnam was not among those present.

The driver and the conductor climbed in together and the bus groaned to a start. There were at least fifteen passengers clinging to the broad steps of the vehicle, making it tilt precariously. If Hansel and Gretel were to be taken to the forest in this bus, they would have an easy time tracing their way back home, following the fumes belched out by the bus.

The bus didn't stop until it reached Manohar Talkies. The regular commuters got in and some unfamiliar people got off. Then there were stops at the clock tower, Minerva Talkies, Ramgopal Statue and Raniganj. And then began the mile-long Tank Bund. This hassle-free run with no stops between seemed to soothe the bus into a smooth crawl. Although Chandru could not see the lake from his perch in the bus, the breeze that played over the waters did not deflect itself from him. The whole bus felt its impartial caress. Tank Bund had changed its appearance periodically with every change of the Nizam's Chief Minister. It was the first thing that struck the eye of every visitor to Hyderabad city and everyone tried his hand at beautifying it. It started with a wall running along the road. Railings rather than a wall, said someone, and the wall was demolished. Then came the changes in those balconies. Let them be brought down to the level of the pavement, said someone else. Sir Mirza Ismail. And so it was demolished; and rebuilt. Beautification of the cities in the princely states seemed to have been an obsession with Sir Mirza Ismail. It was said that he left Mysore a beautiful city. But here in Hyderabad, he lost his ministership too soon to effect much change. He was followed by the Nawab of Chhatari, a man with a moustache that reminded you of a cow's horns. One half of it was pulled out by its roots by Kasim Razvi's Razakars. Poor man, that must have hurt. He left and the one who came after him, the latest in the line, was Laiq Ali. Mountbatten and Sardar Patel were now in Delhi. And India had become free. As had Bhopal and Junagadh. After all that dilly dallying, they had finally opted to join the Indian Union. The Indian tricolour was flying atop Delhi's Red Fort. The day for Bharati's joyous song of liberation in D.K. Pattammal's resonant voice had at last dawned. But here was Hyderabad, still holding out against independent India. The Congress party had organised a join-the-Indian Union Day and someone had managed to secretly hoist the Indian flag at dawn in Sultan Bazaar. The police were in a quandary. 'Bring down the damn thing.'

In the meantime the Razakars and refugees intensified their sloganeering—*Azad Haiderabad rahenga, Lal Quile par chalenga!* On the other hand, there was this Narasimha Rao asking him to put his name in blood to a piece of paper. The bus had crossed the lake. Five minutes, and he should be in college.

Chandru got off the bus at Fateh Maidan along with several others, and the bus left the place. The principal of Nizam College was standing at the college gate. Shorn of the forbidding aura of his own room, he no longer looked like some great mythical hero. Just another person, out in the open. He was herding the students at the gate and on the pavement outside into the college: 'Get in, get in.' The old bicycle keeper was there with him. He would let you escape for a consideration even now. Hyderabad's two-anna bit, a small thin disc less than a half-inch in diameter, was very handy to slip into palms.

Chandru stopped a good distance from the college gate, where he stood undecided. The Nampalli Road, which converted this place into a three-road junction, ran alongside the Fateh Maidan and curved out of sight. There wasn't much traffic on it. A large peepal tree stood at the intersection of the roads. Chandru would have to stand under the tree to catch the bus home. A single large tree amidst the broad paved roads and buildings built to last centuries. No Chief Minister seemed to have ordered it cut down as yet. A police inspector and two constables stood under the tree now.

The 9.55 bell rang and the principal went in. Only a few students now stood with Chandru outside the gate. The inspector kept an eye on them from across the road. Two buses from opposite directions came in and stopped there, and the place became busy again.

Two young men dressed in white kurtas and pyjamas jumped off the compound wall of the Fateh Maidan on to the road. Where had they hidden themselves all this while? They began to cross the road. By the time they reached the college, they had produced Gandhi caps and put them on and chanted *Vande Mataram,* the war cry of the Indian freedom fighters.

Their feeble shouts could not have carried ten feet, but the police inspector was alerted. The young man advanced towards the crowd on the pavement which was now shouting 'Long live India!' and 'Down with police tyranny!' Their shouts had become more strident now.

The inspector gave orders and then all three of them started to cross the road. Just then three motorcycles tore across one after the other, thus delaying the policemen's crossing. Meanwhile, the two young men joined the crowd on the pavement outside the college and they shouted 'We want—' Chandru and the others completed the chant shouting:

'Merger!'

'We want—'

'Merger!'

'Down with—'

'Police tyranny!'

The inspector and the constables had now reached the crowd which began to thin out gradually. When the inspector finally got to the Gandhi-cap men who had started the round of slogan shouting, the rest of the crowd stood at a safe distance.

Chandru watched the faces. The young men were not quite free of fear, nor was the inspector's face without a trace of panic. He caught both the men by their hands and said something like 'Uh huh hum... uh huh hum.' As if in response, the young men stood silent. The inspector swore at all his constables. One of them ran out somewhere. The inspector now addressed the crowd on the pavement, 'Disperse, disperse, please.' Even without waiting for his appeal, the crowd had lost the appearance of a crowd. Some ten or fifteen people stood scattered watching the Gandhi caps and the policemen.

The Gandhi caps were not from Nizam College. One of them kept wiping his face with a handkerchief. If they found this indeterminate wait in the streets in the sun irksome, the policemen found it no less so. At last the policemen who had been rebuked by the inspector returned with a cyclericksha. The inspector asked the Gandhi cap boys to climb into the ricksha, which they did. In the meantime a bicycle was brought for the inspector by another policeman. It must have been the inspector's. He began to ride it and the cyclericksha followed him. The two policemen brought out their bicycles from somewhere and began to follow the cyclericksha. The inspector turned to look at the young men and said pointing to their caps, 'Take them off.' Without a murmur of protest the young men took off their Gandhi caps.

The whole scenario gave Chandru the impression of a play written by a sleepy dramatist. An exciting beginning to achieve something great had fizzled out even as it began. The protesters as well as the police were unsure of themselves.

There were hopes of attending the first hour's class now. The galleries where the science classes were held had only one entrance, and that directly in front of the lecturer's table. English classes were better in this respect, because they were held in the Salar Jung Hall which had about eight doors, allowing you to enter from behind, from the sides as well as from the front. A latecomer could get in unobtrusively, even if he lost his attendance. It would have been a great help if all first periods had been English. Especially at this time when the happenings of the morning were very likely to recur.

Indeed, the past week had been eventful. As had happened today, Chandru was inevitably involved in some of the incidents. The other day Hari Gopal had sent him to watch the fun at the college gate. Chandru asked him to come too but no, he had already seen it all. He had more or less driven Chandru to the gate where there were four girls—women—middle-aged almost. They were driving away anyone who entered the college from the outside. What they said was not clearly audible. He couldn't even make out what language it was. Chandru went through the gate, stood outside the college for a while and went in again. Two women came forward and offered him something. He involuntarily stretched out his hand. They laughed and placed a glass bangle in his open palm. All those who stood by joined in the laughter. They were making fun of him for being effeminate, for attending college—'The State of Hyderabad has refused to join the Indian Union; Swami Ramanand Tirth has been arrested and is now in jail. Thugs led by Kasim Razvi and the Razakars and encouraged by the Nizam are running amok spreading terror in the State. Arms are being smuggled in for these thugs and for the Nizam's forces, and look at this week-kneed man here, he wants to go to college!'

That was the message conveyed by the offer of a woman's bangle to him.

Chandru didn't know what to do with the bangle. If he threw it away, it would be an insult to them. If he put it in his pocket, he would be accepting an insult. He offered it back to them. They laughed. He thrust it into one of the women's hands and ran into the college grounds. He did not attend any class after that but watched the women from a distance. He observed that they didn't offer any bangles to those students who came in with a swagger. Or to those who came by car. All those who dressed loudly were left severely alone. It appeared that protests and boycotts were all meant for those poor persons who lacked the wits to answer back, those for whom life was a struggle even otherwise. They were expected to give up the little they had. If they didn't oblige, they were fair game to be mocked, coerced and compelled into submission. The bell rang, announcing the end of the first period. Relief at last! Chandru went to join his classmates.

2

My debut as a singer among the Tamil residents of Hyderabad, who in those days were a mere three or four thousand, now remains to be chronicled. As was the case with my other assorted acquisitions like the letters of the alphabet, the tables, tip-cat, climbing trees, playing tops or flying kites, my musical training took place with little conscious effort on my part.

It happened when a Mr Alwar started giving music lessons at home to my sisters. For girls, a grounding in classical music was as compulsory an accomplishment as knowing how to wash dishes. Mr Alwar took over the music classes with the same vigour as my mother taught the girls to scour utensils with mud and ash.

I don't remember Mr Alwar as ever being younger than sixty. He had a large knot of hair suspended off the nape of his neck. The general belief was that this heavy knot was meant to keep the rolling of his head within reasonable limits as he sang. He would make his appearance at our house, large bag in hand, some time between seven and eight every morning. Without waiting for anyone, he would spread a mat on the floor and sit down. After about fifteen minutes, my eldest sister would enter, place a harmonium before him and vanish. A further fifteen minutes would pass before my second sister appeared and set down a brass chembu of water to drink. Fifteen minutes again, and my mother would bring him some coffee. After coffee, Alwar would enjoy a leisurely chew of betel leaves and arecanut. Then the lesson would begin with sol-fa exercises in the raga Mayamalavagaula: *sa-ri-ga-ma*. The teacher had to cut in now and again to get them both to keep the same pitch. When the sol-fa was done, they would begin that little song about Ganesha, the one taught to beginners. By now my older sister would be bursting with suppressed giggles. Occasional peals of unprovoked laughter would punctuate her singing and soon infect the other sister as well. Then the teacher would get angry. At this point one would find Mother intervening with a few resounding slaps on the girls' backs. The general melee and the lesson itself would not last beyond nine-fifteen or nine-thirty when we children would gulp down a hasty meal and leave for school. Alwar would be on his way to teach another girl who might live a couple of miles away. How and when Alwar found the time to go home, eat, sleep and look after his family was a mystery. You'd find him at all odd hours of the day, at some house or other, propagating the beginner's raga Mayamalavagaula. If ragas had presiding deities as was believed, the deity of Mayamalavagaula was sure to take care of his needs in the hereafter. As for his needs here and now, he was paid only three rupees per house.

The only occasion that found my older sisters singing was the nine-day festival of dolls, Navaratri, when it is more or less mandatory for girls to sing before the array of dolls. Otherwise, apart from their learning time with Mr Alwar, they were not given to much singing. But the rest of us at home began to sing too. I sang. My younger brother and sisters sang. I even heard my father humming the tune of that little beginners' song.

Mr Alwar's unquestioned supremacy as the music teacher of Secunderabad faced a sudden challenge with the arrival of a new music teacher in the city, a Mr Sundara Bhagavatar. Sundara Bhagavatar sported cropped hair and side burns and wore a gold bordered upper cloth. Alwar, one of the old school, used to teach sol-fa singing first and might not progress beyond it for months or even years. But the new teacher taught full-fledged songs even to beginners. For ears till now used to hearing only meaningless notes of the octave in various permutations and combinations, these songs sounded heavenly. Within a month of his arrival, no less than twenty families had engaged Sundara Bhagavatar.

Sundara Bhagavatar wouldn't come every day. He took only two or three lessons a week. His minimum fee was five rupees. He began by demanding fifteen rupees from us and finally came down to seven, after much bargaining. He had big eyes that were always reddish. His entry into our house would be heralded by a general knocking down of things in his path. If you spread a mat or rug on the floor for him to sit on, he would lift it up by the ends and shake it out with a bang before sitting on it. While he beetled away at the harmonium, the keys kept up a constant tap-tap along with the notes. Self-confidence incarnate, Sundara Bhagavatar awakened the musical sensibilities of the Tamil population of Secunderabad. There were of course those who thought that all he did was degrade public taste. Our Alwar subscribed to this school of thought: 'Look at this man reeking of perfume, teaching children classical songs as if they were folk music. Is that the way to teach music? Shouldn't they be taught the basics? Stop a little girl on the street and repeat a song a few times and she'll surely pick it up. But is that all there is to music? The goddess of music must surely be shedding tears.'

Within two months of replacing the old teacher, all of us at home had graduated to humming the great Tyagaraja's composition, *Sri Rama Padama*. During his lessons, you'd find Sundara Bhagavatar tackling the bellows of the harmonium with every ounce of brute force he could summon, while the fingers of his other hand would hammer away on the keyboard with equal ferocity. He would belt out the song as he played the harmonium: *Sri Rama Padama...* My sisters would scream at the top of their lungs in reply, and the song would be sung at a hurtling speed. Any newcomer chancing upon the scene would be hard put to comprehend what was going on. I'm afraid I may not succeed in conveying to you what was happening in all these homes scattered across the city of Secunderabad during Sundara Bhagavatar's music lessons. Nor would all your powers of imagination—however highly developed—be of much help unless you could also make the necessary connection with medieval jousts and adventures.

Sundara Bhagavatar's spell of spectacular success during which he eclipsed Alwar totally lasted six months after which he made an unannounced exit from Secunderabad. It transpired that he owed money everywhere: to the milkman, grocer, landlord. Once it became clear that it was no use waiting for him, Alwar was reappointed to teach several of his old pupils. The interlude benefited Alwar—his rates went up. He stopped spending hours at each tuition. And it was no more than three lessons a week now.

Music in Secunderabad followed neither Alwar's style nor Sundara Bhagavatar's. Each house cultivated its own distinctive dismal style of singing.

And thus it began to be said, 'Why, Chandru sings quite well. Not bad at all.' I believed it myself though I was too young them to distinguish between good and bad music and my circumstances didn't allow me to find out for certain. I learnt songs by listening avidly to the Madras station on our Philco radio. Madras could be heard only at night and that amidst a lot of disturbance. I picked up a few songs with simple tunes this way, but remembering the words of songs was not easy. To make matters worse, the singers would swallow half the words and mutilate the rest. I remember a Tamil song in support of the Indian National Congress sung by a famous musician of the day, Musiri, which I used to sing often. But my version had liquid sounds in the place of nasals, which made gibberish out of high patriotism. It was a long time before I deciphered the words of the original.

In an unprecedented move, our school, which till then had Telugu or Urdu speaking headmasters, suddenly appointed a Tamil enthusiast from the Tamil districts as headmaster. This should not have occasioned any surprise as our school was founded by a Tamil family. But having lived for three generations in the Nizam's State, what the present generation of the family spoke was not strictly Tamil; it was a curious mixture of tongues. Among those huge portraits of our patrons in the school hall, Somasundara Mudaliar and Hanumanta Rao were repeated quite often. Some honorary title or other like Diwan Bahadur, Rao Bahadur or Rao Sahib was attached to every name. All of them sported brocade caps or turbans, moustache, a daub of holy ashes, sandalwood and vermilion on their foreheads and a pocket watch with the chain showing. One was an equestrian figure. Another—the only name preceded by a 'Sir'—had a sword hanging from his waist.

I often stood in front of this picture, lost in contemplation of the sword.

Though established by a Tamil family, no more than a hundred students in this school out of a total of a thousand were Tamil. The new headmaster—he was called the principal—got acquainted with each of the one hundred.

With the new principal came new rules in the running of the school, like closing the gate after the third bell in the morning, and opening them in the evening only five minutes before closing time. During our prayer meetings, a teacher was asked to address the students every week. All the classes were to take turns singing Tagore's song on India, *Jana gana mana,* each class singing it for a week. The final touch was that the new principal started a Tamil Association in the school and ordered all students including Telugu and Urdu boys to attend its meetings. The inaugural meet of the association was held one fine afternoon at three. No classes were held during the last period.

I sat with the rest of my class on a sheet spread on the floor of the hall. The crowded hall had only a single fan whirring straight above the dais. But we were at an age when the body did not seem to mind the heat and the stuffiness.

It was four o'clock when the principal made his appearance along with the chairman and secretary of the school committee. These two men wore a brocade cap and a turban respectively, but the principal's cropped head was uncovered.

The principal spoke first, welcoming the two guests. His speech was in chaste Tamil, something we had never heard in our city. Even our Tamil teachers generously sprinkled their speech with Urdu words like 'jaldi' and Telugu words like 'jitam'. It was always 'jaldi vaa' for 'come quickly'. Telugu also came in handy when we had to be scolded.

After his speech in praise of the founders, patrons and office-bearers of the school, the principal announced: 'Now we shall have a prayer song.' And then he called out, 'Chandra-sekharan!'

A deep silence hung over the hundreds of students sitting on the floor, the dozens of teachers standing along the wall and the three on the dais.

I looked about to find out who was being called. A few small bodies wriggled but no one stood up. Our Tamil pandit, who was standing some distance away, caught my eye and said, '*Ai* Chandrasekharan, he's calling you.' I still looked round.

But now, well-aimed punches caught my back and waist from the boys sitting close to me. The Tamil pandit took a few rapid strides towards me. 'Go on, sing,' he said. I got up. The pandit shoved me forward with a 'Go!'. And I embarked upon the journey to the dais, a seemingly interminable one.

The shirt I had on that day was too short for me. Through its split ends on either side my waist was visible, along with the bulge formed by the rolling up of the extra length of my shorts. It was there for all to see, I don't know if they did see it. With my hands pulling down the shirt, I began to inch forward. My shorts were too big for me and kept flapping like those billowing full skirts worn by the gopis, the milkmaids who danced with Krishna. I felt a cool wind blow up the flaring shorts and freeze my stomach. I managed to reach the dais. Just one step but I stumbled and my head rested on the secretary's lap. The sesame oil I had applied to my hair must have stained his trousers.

I looked from the dais at the vast ocean of humanity before me. Each pair of eyes pinched me all over. Krishnaswamy's fumed with venom. All his brothers, the boys I had known, not known, those I had seen but not known, those I had not seen at all... In that corner Balwant Singh who was in my class and who constantly harassed me with his pea-shooter from the back bench now riddled me with his eyes. The kittenish growth of hair from his turban was now on its way to his throat. Did they pity me for my predicament or envy my sudden importance? This vast turbulence lay before me, seething with expectation. If only I could drown and disappear.

'Sing a song,' said the principal, 'sing something devotional.' He had a broad face with a forest of a moustache on it, a potential lair for lions, tigers, pythons.

'Sing, boy, sing.'

The secretary, the chairman, the principal, all of them waited for me. I wondered who had done this to me. Which implacable enemy of mine could have told the principal I could sing?

The moment was inescapable. It might lengthen into hours or eons and I would still be standing there, incapable of bringing it to a close. There was no way of avoiding it without singing. Oh why was it that my eyes could still see and my ears could hear! I was still conscious, I could follow what was being said.

'Come on now. How long are you going to stand there? Can't you sing a prayer?'

'Maybe he can sing only film songs,' said the secretary. The three of them laughed.

I felt a little less tense now, shifting from one foot to the other. Oh for a song, a song! A song did flash through my mind. *Sri Rama Padama*. But I didn't want to sing it. It was somehow inseparable from Sundara Bhagavatar, the harmonium and my sisters. Sundara Bhagavatar sitting cross-legged on the floor, keeping time with his hand beating his thigh, or his thigh bashing the floor, and my sisters erupting into a volcano of notes sung at high speed. All this was the proper milieu of *Sri Rama Padama*. If the principal had offered to play the harmonium perhaps I could have had a go at the song.

But I did sing something in the end. I had no idea what I was singing until the first line was out of my lips. It turned out to be a love song. The secretary was quite right—it was a song from a film, from *Sakuntalai*. It was sung by the heroine after her meeting with her lover Dushyanta. I hadn't seen the film, though. It had been released only recently and was not worn enough to reach our city. I had learnt to sing a garbled version of the song by listening to it on our radio.

The song began with a reference to the belief that the twitching of the left shoulder and eye was a harbinger of future joy for a girl.

I proceeded to sing it at great speed, slurring over the words and leaving out parts, reached the end of the song somehow and got off the dais. When I walked back to my place, there was absolute silence in the hall. No one seemed to know what had happened.

The secretary stood up to make his speech. Unable to find my class and my row, I stepped on the thighs and on the legs of a new set of boys and sat down somewhere. The boys kept pushing and hissing but I was in a trance, fidgeting restlessly yet with no will of my own.

The major part of the secretary's half-hour-long speech was devoted to fulsome praise of my 'devotional' song. The poor man didn't know it was a song from a film. Nor did I for that matter, at that point of time. All those details about who sang it, when and in which film was knowledge which lay in the future. Possibly the secretary had never heard any Tamil songs before. Though aware that there were songs in films, he was innocent of any knowledge of *Sakuntalai,* the classic of Tamil cinema which was bewitching audiences in the southern parts of the country. Even those famous initials MS and GNB, must have meant nothing to him beyond being letters of the English alphabet. They happened to represent the initials of the actress and the actor who played the leading roles in this film. That could easily explain why he praised my song. He went on to give us some advice as well about the words of the song. Since the first line of the song suggested that the singer was a woman, it could be made more suitable for a boys' school like ours, he said, by changing the words of the song, the twitching of the right shoulder and eye rather than the left, since for a boy a twitch on the right side brought good luck. I didn't expect the secretary's praise of my musical abilities to have any long-term repercussions, though I did go round with a sort of ghost-stricken mien for the rest of the day, eyes unfocussed and unblinking. At home I was made to swallow a pepper brew, a home remedy you can't escape, whatever the nature of your illness, whether a stomachache, sprain or a hard blow on the head. A few days later, at school, I was told by our watchman Gangaram that the principal wanted to see me. Gangaram was the least sickly looking of the three or four odd-job men employed by our school. He spoke a kind of Maharashtrian Urdu. By the time I deciphered his message and reached the principal's room it was fifteen minutes past closing time. All those big buildings and playgrounds were hushed and deserted. The principal was not in his room.

I stood there and took in every inch of the room. The cupboards were full of shields, cups and scrolls all covered with the patina of age. Maps of the world, India, the British Isles and the State of Hyderabad, and a few charts of the human anatomy, hung on the wall.

There was also a picture of a man with his skin peeled off as it were revealing his muscles and nerves. Then there was a skeleton and a few bones. Three long canes in a corner. Books and notebooks. Our teachers should be made to write essays, I thought, and the Principal should correct them. He should score out the teachers' work with crooked red lines and crossmarks all over. He should tear off their exercises, crumple the pages and fling the notebooks at the wall. Yes, justice demanded it.

'What do you want?'

The voice struck me with fear. I turned and saw that the principal had come into the room.

'What do you want? What's your name? he asked again.

'Gangaram—' I began but couldn't continue.

'Oh, you're Chandrasekharan, aren't you? The one who sang that prayer?'

'Yes, sir.'

'I had asked you to come yesterday.'

'But sir, Gangaram told me only now.'

'Do you know who else sings in our school?'

'Sir?'

'Do you know any boy who can sing, you know, sing songs?'

It was some time before I grasped his question. Then I said, Jagan can sing, sir. Jagannathan, the scout. He sings at every campfire.'

'What sorts of songs?'

'Telugu songs, Urdu songs.'

'Not Tamil songs?'

'He is a Telugu boy, sir.'

'I want boys who can sing in Tamil.'

'There aren't many, sir.'

'I heard that Varadachari's son sings.'

'Who is that, sir?'

'Anyone else you can think of?'

'Our Tamil pandit, sir.'

The principal laughed. 'Do you call that music?'

I said nothing. The Tamil pandit used to sing *Tirukkural, Tirikadukam* and every other piece of Tamil poetry to the same tune during our Tamil classes. It didn't sound bad at all to me.

'Our Tamil boys,' he announced, 'should put up a play.' I stayed silent.

The topics on the principal's agenda that day were not such as to facilitate easy comprehension. He continued, 'It appears that this school has never put up any Tamil play till now. Telugu plays, even English plays, but no Tamil plays. Hereafter, we must put up one or two Tamil plays every year.' I stood listening like someone who had nothing to do with the subject discussed.

'This year we must put up *Karnan.*' He went on, 'I have the book with me. There are only three singing parts—Karna, his mother and Krishna. You could be Karna's mother. We'd still need two boys for Karna and Krishna. You're too short to be one of the men, you see.'

The subject had indeed taken on a sudden personal relevance. I also sensed that the situation was fraught with the gravest danger for me. I had somehow managed to sing something once. But to sing a lot of songs one after the other on a stage, and that dressed as a woman! At that moment the figures of all those in this wide world, including those at home, who disliked me and would gloat over my discomfiture raced through my mind. And I shuddered to think of the reaction in Lancer Barracks to the news of my acting in a play.

'Anyway, let me know if you can think of any boy. I shall go around myself to the classes and find out.' Then he asked, 'By the way, does Sundaram come to your house regularly?'

'Who's that, sir?'

'The music master, Sundaram?'

I decided that Sundaram was none other than Mr Sundara Bhagavatar. I also deduced the identity of the culprit who had informed the principal about my musical pretensions.

We did manage to stage that Tamil play. We even sold a lot of tickets. The Tamil population of Secunderabad turned out in full strength for the show. We put it on for two days. I wore a white sari on the first day and a black one on the second. If any sympathy had been expected for the widow, my taking her part took care of that. My widow's clothes caused great mirth. Whenever I appeared on the stage, everyone laughed, even those who had never laughed in their lives before and might never laugh again. Only Mother didn't laugh. She avoided my eyes throughout the play. I made five appearances in all, singing a song at every appearance besides which I also had to enter and exit singing. There was also a musical conversation between Karna and me. I began with 'You are my son, you are my son, you are indeed my son,' to which he replied, 'You are my mother, you are my mother, you are indeed my mother'.

Karna, the great warrior friend of Duryodhana, was a foundling brought up by a charioteer. And this scene on the eve of the Mahabharata was the one we put on, his first meeting with his mother who had abandoned him as soon as he was born. So I had to reveal myself as Karna's mother and he acknowledged me. However, refusing to desert his friend Duryodhana, Karna gave me, his mother, his word that he would not attack any of my sons except Arjuna. He also promised not to use the deadly arrow Nagastra more than once. I had to promise in return that if Karna fell in battle, I would cry over his body. But that turned out to be a tall order, for the crying had to be done musically in a song set to Bilahari. So when my widow's white was replaced by a black sari for the second day's performance, I also took the liberty of changing the song. I changed my crying, rather.

This experience in improvising stood me in good stead in my college years. When the Tamil Association of Nizam College (which had no more than eighteen members) compelled me to practise a song in praise of the Mother goddess for its inauguration, I replaced it at the last moment with poet Bharati's freedom song *Viduthalai, Viduthalai!* which was a proclamation of freedom and equality to every caste and creed, man and woman, to every Indian. It was on the following day that 'Join Indian Union Day' rallies were held throughout Hyderabad. Within a week, on 15 August 1947, India became independent. The Indian National Congress was banned in the whole State of Hyderabad but it continued its activities from Bombay with Jayaprakash Narayan as its chief adviser. Narasimha Rao, my friend in college, a Telugu boy, took me to meet Kasi Nath Vaidya, a Hyderabad Congress leader whose presence in the city was unknown to the police. Narasimha Rao translated the Tamil freedom song I had sung into Telugu for the leader's benefit. The leader said that the poem deserved to be sung all over the State as a song of revolution. And I began to be considered a revolutionary by a few.

3

Professor Ranga's Shakespeare class in the Salarjung Hall. He began with the line 'Old John of Gaunt...'. 'Old John of Gaunt'. This was the name the students had given him, and it caused a brief ripple in the class which soon subsided, and then the back rows began to doze, heads resting on the desktops.

Chandru sat in the last row. Professor Ranga had this habit of looking at those in the front rows and talking as if he was conducting a conversation with them. These rows bore the brunt of the deeds of Bolingbroke and Mowbray. Many chairs in the rows were vacant. Students like Chandru always rushed in and occupied the back seats when the classes began, but Professor Ranga didn't bother much about these preferences of the students. After the first five minutes which he spent taking attendance, he would devote the next fifty-five minutes to a dramatic reading of *Richard II* from the book. In the past six classes they had been stuck with the first act. Every class started from the very beginning of the play—'Old John of Gaunt'.

But for the faint tapping of the typewriters in the college office next to the hall, there were no other noises to break the drone of the professor's voice. There was an occasional distant hooting of a car on the street outside the college.

Masood, who sat next to Chandru in the class, and Anwar Ali Khan, the boy on the bench in front, were both sound asleep. They both wore sherwani jackets of such fine material that you were tempted to feel it. These signs of affluence were, as a rule, most in evidence during English classes because English was common to both the science and history sections. The science students, boys and girls alike, made you feel that they were here to study, and study they must. You found them moping, backs bent, brows knit and shabbily dressed. But high spirits, affluence and leisure marked the lives of the history students. Most of the cars that came to the campus were for the history students. They appropriated the lion's share of the college sports equipment. They were the ones who took part in the elocution contests. Theirs were the cheers and applause during the mock parliament sessions. The vice-president and secretary of the college students union were from the history group.

Masood turned his head in sleep, causing Chandru's book to fall down from the desk. He muttered a 'Sorry dost' to Chandru, picked up the book lazily with a long hand reaching down and promptly went to sleep again, his well-fed, hefty shoulders moving up and down in a slow and steady rhythm. Silky fuzz had begun to cover his cheeks but his face was still that of a child. Sitting beside him Chandru felt old and hoary, though his bulk was half that of Masood.

Professor Ranga was lecturing on the prominence of dramatic irony in Shakespeare. John of Gaunt, who endears himself to King Richard, later falls from favour. Still later, the king, who has exercised powers of imprisonment, banishment and confiscation over his subjects loses his throne and finds himself in prison. The King's words at this point are as poignant as John of Gaunt's. But the fact of the matter was that Professor Ranga's lament was more poignant. 'John of Gaunt emerges as one of the most famous patriots in Shakespeare's play. An old man out of favour with the king becomes a great patriot. One wonders if his last breath was reserved for his country or his dear son... Poor John of Gaunt!'

Chandru's attention wandered from Professor Ranga. He looked round. Boys and girls. A little over a hundred of them. More than half the students were in trousers and jackets, only because the college insisted on it. There were possibly many among them who had just this set of clothes, crumpled, dirty, torn and patched. There were no special regulations concerning the girls' dress. All of them wore saris. The girls' saris provided a mine of information about the wearer's lifestyle, just as the quality of the boys' clothes did. Take Masood's sherwani. It gave you a fairly accurate idea as to what his house was like, what food he ate and how much he ate, how many servants he had and also what his father's views were since last November. If he were to hear John of Gaunt's speech, he would favour certain groups in Hyderabad and spurn certain others. Masood himself, notwithstanding his being six foot tall and two broad, would not be as prejudiced as his father. But, think of what happened the other day. God, what a ball of hate Masood had been then!

It had happened about a week ago. There was great excitement during lunch hour in college. All the colleges in Hyderabad had decided to conduct a joint procession to press for people's representation in the Nizam's State Government. Police permission had been obtained for this rally, ostensibly meant to voice the people's aspirations.

But as the students left the college, the real motivation for the demonstration became apparent. The students dispersed and regrouped themselves like the colours in a kaleidoscope. All the sherwani-jackets gathered together. Those in shirts-pyjamas and coats gravitated towards one another. For those in sherwanis lessons would continue as before in college. The principal and the professors were waiting near the college buildings or on the verandas. They had never been as visible as today. Figures of authority whose mere presence was enough to evoke obedience, they now stood out in the open, bereft of their protective roofs, uncertain and weak. They were aware that their high visibility today was likely to weaken their authority among the students for ever. Professor Ranga was there. Mohammad Ghani was there. The Tamil pandit was there. And so was the principal.

A small procession came in from Basheer Bagh, and the Nizam College students joined them. They were strangers to each other, and the two groups maintained a slight demarcation. The leaders of the procession couldn't have been students. They looked too grown up. The procession went forward along the left of the road. The Hyderabad Police were everywhere.

No slogans were chanted. The only noise was the shuffling of feet. On Abid Road, the procession became longer. Abid Road was where the Palace Cinema was. There was a wide flight of more than twenty steps leading up to the cinema hall from the street. The building must have been built in the days when labour was cheap and building materials were available in plenty. You could easily mistake it for a palace if you didn't already know that it was a cinema. *Anmol Ghadi* was on today. Those who had come to see the film crowded the steps and watched while policemen armed with batons ordered off the processionists. But then was it a joke or did it mean something more to them? Those who came to the afternoon shows, especially for a Hindi film, belonged to a certain class. They were drawn from various religious groups, true, but classwise, they were more or less homogeneous. These were the people given to walking over the chairs in the hall, smoking all the time, spitting, scratching themselves and whistling at various pitches whenever there was a break in the film. They were not the sort to be satisfied with being mere spectators. Neither were these the sort of days which kept them satisfied. If you thought about what happened at the stunt film *Punjab Mail*. The film mostly comprised the antics of the hero and the heroine who careered around on the screen. The corpulent heroine Nadia would jump up and land effortlessly on a roof two floors above, while John Cavas swinging on chandeliers would descend accurately on his horse from a great height and gallop away shouting 'Hey'. A Congress flag happened to be shown somewhere in the film and a picture of Gandhi in another part. At once, wolf whistles became shouts and screams and the film had to be stopped. Any tricolour found or seen anywhere was instantly brought down and torn to pieces those days in Hyderabad. *Anmol Ghadi*, the film now showing, was about a pair of childhood lovers who grow into adulthood and having nothing better to do, go on loving. It was an innocuous film with Noorjahan breaking into song every now and then with thoughts of her lover Surendra; Surendra would likewise break into song thinking of Noorjahan. Suraiya would sing thinking of both of them.

The procession had grown greatly in size by the time it reached Sultan Bazaar. There were as many others in it now as there were students. The Sultan Bazaar locality had seen frequent police lathi charges in the past four or five months and three people had died. It was here that the Indian tricolour was hoisted on the eve of the Indian Independence, and when 15 August dawned the flag was seen flying. The police were embarrassed and went round the city through the day in a sheepish huff; no one knew who had hoisted the flag. Then there was a clash with a crowd, followed by Section 144, a lathi charge, teargas and stabbings. These events had reverberations in Secunderabad as well. Chandru ran his fingers over his forehead. The procession inched along through very narrow and congested lanes that had been honoured with the name 'street'. The procession was about to cross a small bridge, the Lakdi Ka Pul across the Musi river. The plan was to hold a meeting at the open ground on the other side of the bridge. A posse of policemen with some senior police officials stood about a hundred yards before the bridge. Their presence brought the procession to a halt.

The sun beat down mercilessly. As long as the procession moved, there had been gaps in it, but now the ranks closed in tightly. Even as the police surrounded them, a message passed through the crowd—permission for the meeting had been refused, but the leaders were trying to get it even now. The meeting must be held, it had to be held, whatever the cost. No matter how late it got, there had to be a meeting. Sit down, all of you. Please sit down. Wherever you are on the street, sit down.

A few were already dropping out. They had realised the seriousness of the situation. Chandru was not familiar with this locality. Where should he go to catch a bus home? The people here were not like the people in Secunderabad. They had an alien look. There was no concrete building in sight, only mud-walled structures which looked like huts but which were not as convenient with their low and narrow openings for doorways. An open gutter in front with its slime and pong, dogs and pigs, hens and ducks. The houses had torn sacking for curtains. God knew how many hundreds crowded behind those sack-cloth curtains, inured to dirt and disease. Did religion have any relevance here at all? Yet these were the places where every communal riot took its toll, houses were looted, possessions were burnt and skulls cracked.

Chandru squatted on the street, a bare ten feet behind the front row, facing the group of helmeted policemen. They carried lathis—well-polished, shiny black sticks. Bloodstains wouldn't show on the black surface. Were these polished with blood by any chance? There was only a muffled noise to be heard. All traffic had come to a stop. Chandru turned to look behind and found that a part of the street was filled with the processionists, all sitting. A lot of police caps and lathis were seen at the back as well. What was happening? Where had all those people gone, those who had led the procession? How long could this calm last, with the procession now shrunk to an island surrounded by police?

Four police officers spluttered past on two motorcycles along the length of the procession. The next step would be a lathi-charge. Fear began to cover those who sat there, like molten tar.

Chandru looked round, frightened. There were people crushing him on all sides, but not a single familiar face. There had been at least fifty of his college friends with him when they had started. Had they slipped away? Or were they caught somewhere else in this crowd? What madness had led him on? Was he going to fall amidst strangers in a strange place, his skull broken?

A few people in the front row were trying to say something to the policemen, but at the slightest movement, a policeman waved his baton and shouted 'Sit down!'. It would take him only a minute to knock down the intervening heads and reach Chandru.

A police officer with a preoccupied look now approached the front of the procession and surveyed those sitting on the ground. His eyes halted at every face. Chandru locked eyes with him for a second. Brass buttons shone bright on his starched uniform. All those coloured stripes on his shirt seemed to proclaim him an experienced officer. He must have a family, children. Was he looking for his own son in the crowd?

A police truck now appeared on the scene and policemen in a different kind of uniform jumped out. The tear gas squad was here. Most of them wore masks. Now was the time for the processionists to decide—should they disperse, or stay and be beaten up?

There was a sudden commotion in the crowd, though everyone continued to sit. Stay where you are. Lie down on the street even if it means death. But why did young boys have to become the target of batons? They should be allowed to go. No, they shouldn't. Sit where you are. If the police start hitting you, lie down on the street.

Some start to weep. A few young boys near Chandru cry out for their parents: 'Amma! Appa! Save me!' They place their schoolbags on their heads. Someone says, 'Dip your handkerchief in water—it's the best thing for tear gas.' But where was the water? Even the Musi river was now just two streaks of water on its dry bed, as if someone had lanced it across. Anyway, the river was quite far off. One couldn't run there without getting hit. It was impossible to run at all in this crowd. He was trapped.

The tear gas squad stood in formation. Police whistles sounded from all sides and the loudspeakers blared in Urdu: 'Disperse in three minutes. You have just three minutes in which to disperse.'

The demonstrators who had sat as a disciplined group until now begin to run amuck. There is some attempt to control the general stampeding, but there is no stopping them any more. They run everywhere, staggering and falling and getting up. Chandru screamed 'Amma!' as he felt a rough shod foot on his back. Then he got up and started to run.

He had no idea where he was heading. The roar of the procession was still strident because of the adults in it. There were policemen in front and on the right. A row of small dwellings lined the left side of the street. The gaps between the houses were already filled with people, with more and more trying to squeeze in.

The first shell burst. A wave of foul smell and a column of smoke. Eyes began to burn and shrieks filled the air—Amma! Amma! Chandru dashed blindly towards a lane, not stopping to pick up the books that fell from his hand. Hundreds of men pressed forward from behind. If it turned out to be a blind alley, they couldn't all get in. On an impulse, Chandru poked a hand through a sack-cloth curtain and pushed. There was a door behind the screen which gave way. He let himself in, closed the door behind him and forced himself into a mud house. A modest place but a house all the same. Just behind the door was a washing place with a few battered old aluminium vessels. The puddle of dirty water at the mouth of the drain was covered with flies. Two hens scurried away flapping their wings. A figure was now visible inside the house, an old woman. She was emaciated and the cloth she wore couldn't possibly absorb any more grime. She opened her mouth. The upper front teeth were missing, the rest of the teeth large and stained. Before she could scream, Chandru extended his arms in a gesture of begging—no, she did not scream.

Masood couldn't have any inkling of all that was happening. Nor could all those others, those sherwani-clad people. But the way Masood and his friends looked at the students in the procession the next day was eloquent with contempt—so you think the likes of you can overthrow our Nizam, do you?

Chandru had seen the Nizam twice, both times as he passed them on the street. The police used to whistle down all traffic to a stop whenever the Nizam's car passed, mostly on a visit to the mosque. The Nizam would be sitting in a corner of the back seat, a shrivelled up figure occupying a tiny fraction of the seat.

Dislodging this man shouldn't prove much of a feat even for Chandru. This Nizam, His Exalted Highness Mir Usman Ali Khan Bahadur blah blah blah and that toothless old woman may have been brother and sister in some earlier birth. But then, Muslims don't have rebirths, do they? Even so, the old woman had an amazing likeness to the Nizam. Not that it would make any difference to her whether she was ruled by a Nizam or a Shivaji or an Asoka. Though not a beggar, she lived in degrading poverty, squalor and starvation, like the generations before her and after her. She could have been brought down with a blow of a breath or killed with a single blow of the hand. But she had understood his entreaty. She had not betrayed him to the police. But for her, Chandru would have been among the fifteen or so people whose heads had been broken that day. But Masood? Masood had a way of knowing all that.

Professor Ranga was going on and on about Shakespeare. John of Gaunt's wisdom, patience, tolerance and patriotism. Patriotism that had survived service under an arrogant king. John of Gaunt, an aristocrat related to the king, must have enjoyed all the good things of life in his time, mused Chandru. What about the poor people of those times, people like this poor old woman who must have formed the majority of the population? Would they too have declaimed themselves like John of Gaunt, spouting philosophy, idealism, advice? Were persons like them ever heard to speak? Did that old woman of Hyderabad ever have a voice? If Shakespeare chose to make her speak, would he leave out the punning and obfuscating? Would it still be two meanings a word and four explanations a sentence?

Chandru clasped his hands tightly to his forehead as if to contain an explosion. He leaned forward and laid his head on the desk. Masood opened his eyes and winked at Chandru, his head still on the desk. Chandru turned his face away. Masood gave Chandru's ear a slow twist. Chandru turned, bridling, and said 'Leave me alone, will you?'

'Come now, don't get cross with me, friend,' said Masood in tones of endearment. And winked again. It was no ordinary wink.

The class was over. It was time for the science and history sections to go their different ways. Chandru overtook Masood and walked quickly towards the science block. Two teams were at a game of cricket on the playing fields.

Chandru told himself—in future, don't run away. Don't ever.

4 |

The impact of *Vidutalai,* the Tamil song on freedom that I sang, was beyond all my expectations. The meetings of the Tamil association of our college used to be the least attended. The Telugu and Urdu association meetings always found the hall full to overflowing, but the Tamil meetings were mostly addressed to vacant chairs. A few students from other groups would come and sit with us for the first ten or fifteen minutes and then leave. Of the few Tamil-speaking teachers in our college, none except the Tamil pandit came to the Tamil meetings. The principal, being the president of all college associations, would adorn the central chair on the dais for five minutes. Not for a moment did I realise that Professor Tambimuthu was among those present when I sang about freedom: 'Vidutalai'. How could I when I was in a state of delirium throughout, call it ecstasy if you think the word also suggests an uncontrollable tremor of the mind and body. When Professor Tambimuthu smiled at me, my first thought as usual was that it must be meant for someone else, but it wasn't. Professor Tambimuthu taught us chemistry. I was not on smiling terms with anyone on the staff. In fact, I had become so adept at hiding myself that you could have pointed me out as an exemplar of anonymity. But there were occasions that challenged my claims to anonymity and here was one in the shape of Professor Tambimuthu. That evening found me standing in his room.

'Well, well, you're a Tamil boy, are you?' he said in Tamil and wanted to know my name. Mind you, I had been his student for well over four months. Besides, I had once broken the stopper of the jar containing hydrogen sulphide making the whole class pinch their noses and run. Besides which I also shared my table and cupboard with the only presentable girl in the group. To crown it all, I had made this Tambimuthu himself call me an idiot. Despite all that, I seemed to have somehow managed to keep my name hidden from him. Anyway, I told him my name now.

'I didn't know you could sing,' he said.

My thoughts went back to the principal of my high school. He had begun the interview in much the same fashion. And then he had gone on to put me on the stage in a saree and had watched the fun.

'What song was that?' Professor Tambimuthu asked.

'Which one sir?'

'The one you sang on Tamil Day.'

'You mean *Vidutalai* sir?'

'Ah, yes. Say it again.'

'Vidutalai.'

'Sing it now.'

'Here, sir?'

'Yes.'

'Now, sir?'

'Yes now. Is it getting late for you to go home?'

'Yes sir... No sir'

'Won't take you more than two minutes, my boy. It was wonderful that day, you know'.

'I don't know sir.'

'Now get on with it.'

So I sang *Vidutalai* in that chemistry room haunted by spirits of Egyptian alchemists and Madame Curie, a curious amalgam altogether.

'Well, write it down for me, will you?'

I blinked as usual. 'Sir, this is a Tamil song. It can only be written in Tamil.'

'And you think I don't know Tamil?'

'No sir... All right, sir.'

I tore a sheet from the chemistry practicals notebook and wrote the song down, correcting lines that had sounded wrong when I sang, and in the process spoilt the lines that had been correct. Professor Tambimuthu took the sheet in his hand and scrutinised it.

'May I go now, sir?'

'What's the hurry, sit down.'

I continued to stand. I was afraid he might leave the subject of my singing and move on to my lessons. Also, my thoughts were with *Coverley Papers*, our set text for that year. For some obscure reason, the boys' nickname for Tambimuthu was Will Honeycomb. You may remember that he was the worthless son of a noble family, vain and fond of hunting and women.

'Sing it again,' said the professor.

'Again, sir?'

'Yes. Again.'

I took the sheet back from him, because I had written my own version of the song in it, and it wouldn't do to change the words while I sang again. This time, he joined me in the singing. I felt uncomfortable. What if somebody should hear our duet? While I sang nervously off-key, the professor himself didn't seem to be a great believer in sticking to any pitch. So between ourselves, we produced the whole range of sounds that the human voice was capable of. Professor

Tambimuthu was extremely happy. I had never imagined that music had such powers. He confessed, 'This is the first time ever that I'm singing a Tamil song.'

'Shall I go now, sir?'

'Wait. Why are you in such a great hurry? Can't you get a bus at this time?'

'I've come by bicycle, sir.'

'That makes it easier still. You can go whenever you please. Now, I'm going to sing the song by myself. See if it's all right.'

And Professor Tambimuthu sang. He explored all those domains of music the rest of us could never have known existed. In the last line of the song each repetition of the thrice repeated word 'Vidutalai' rises higher than the last and I had taught him to strike a really high note at the conclusion. Tambimuthu's voice didn't go very high though his eyeballs kept rolling higher and higher.

Then he asked me proudly, 'Was that all right?'

'Yes sir,' I lied.

'I pick up songs at the first hearing. As for this song, I've been singing it ever since I heard you that day.'

I didn't say anything.

'Whose lyric is this?' he asked.

'Bharati's.'

'Who?'

'Bharati, sir'

'Who's he? Is he alive now?'

The only thing I knew at that time about the greatest Tamil poet of this century was that *Kalki* magazine had started a collection for a memorial to be built in his name in Ettayapuram, his birth place. Long lists of donors—several pages of it—were published week after week in this magazine, I knew more about these people than about the poet. My father had donated some money as well, and his name had appeared in the lists. My knowledge of twentieth century Tamil literature was confined to the Tamil weeklies *Ananda Vikatan* and *Kalki* which appeared late in our city. It seemed that Tamil migrants like Tambimuthu had lost even that sort of contact with Tamil. I wondered when his people had migrated to Hyderabad.

So there we were, Tambimuthu and I, in the year of Indian Independence, paying homage to our national poet by singing his song of freedom.

'A wonderful song,' said Professor Tambimuthu, 'To think I wouldn't have known about it, if you hadn't sung it that day.'

'I know two more songs, sir, Actually I had wanted to sing one of the two that day, but they're a bit long.'

'Will you teach them to me?'

'Not today, sir.'

'No. Some other time. And look here'.

'Yes sir.'

'Don't tell anyone.'

I didn't know what it was I was not to tell.

'I mean... about my learning the song.'

'All right, sir.' And then I made a big blunder. I said, 'Even Telugu people want to learn this song, sir.'

'I see... Who?'

'Narasimha Rao, sir.'

'Who's Narasimha Rao?'

'A student in the A batch, sir. A Congress leader.'

At the mention of Congress, the professor's face clouded over.

'Be careful. Don't mix with them.'

'But that may not be possible, sir.'

Professor Tambimuthu stiffened. 'I tell you this because you are a Tamil boy. Don't get mixed up in all this.'

'But I have even given my signature, sir.' I showed him my finger.

'What?'

'We put down our names in blood, sir.'

'What nonsense!'

I took warning. 'Can I go now, sir?'

'What's all this about signatures?'

I stood silent. He won't sing any more freedom songs, I thought.

'What was that about signatures?'

'We've been made to take a pledge, sir.'

'What pledge?' Tambimuthu rebuked me sharply, standing up.

'We're going to demonstrate in front of the college from the first of December.'

'Get out! Get out!'

I darted to the door. But before I was out, the professor called out, 'Chandrasekhar!'

I turned to look at him.

'Come here.'

I went to his table again. He went and closed the door, plunging the darkening room into further darkness. Dusk was falling outside.

'Tell me the whole thing.' I stood determined not to tell him anything, and he sensed it. 'Look, Chandrasekhar,' he said, 'I don't want you to go to the dogs. Let the others do what they like. If there is another strike or demonstration, the trouble-makers will be rusticated.'

I didn't know the exact meaning of 'rustication', but I knew it must be some sort of punishment.

'Trust me and tell me. It'll stand you in good stead later on.'

My resolve weakened and I told him how I went with Narasimha Rao to meet the leader of the Hyderabad State Congress, that I had been distributing pamphlets among students known to me.

'Do you have any on you now?'

'No sir.'

'What was the pamphlet about?'

I gave him some details. Digambar Rao Bindu had had a meeting with Vallabhbhai Patel in Delhi and it was decided that the college students of Hyderabad should intensify their struggle against the oppression of the Nizam–Razakar combine. The first step was a two-page pledge followed by signatures and there had been fifteen who had signed with me. In blood. I nicked my finger and blood spurted out. Besides me, three other students dipped their pens in my blood and signed. Compared with the pledge written in ink, the names in blood were dim, nearly illegible. Blood didn't seem to be proper material for writing on paper.

I had never seen Professor Tambimuthu in such a sombre mood. 'Were any girls involved?'

'Yes sir. A few. But none from our college.'

'Did you sign because of the girls?'

'Oh no sir. It wasn't like that.'

Professor Tambimuthu stood up. 'I promise not to report this,' he said. 'But I can tell that it's not going to do you any good. Idealism is a good thing, no doubt. Don't I have it myself? Why do you think I learnt this song on freedom from you? Inspiring, indeed. But then, this is no place for idealism. Look at me. I've been in this college for twenty years. Yet, when I asked for a year's leave to go to England, I was asked to resign my job and go. I should have been made the vice-principal long ago, but I wasn't even considered for the post. If I recommended a student for a scholarship, he would be the first to be rejected. To survive in this place one must wear a red cap or a turban. Mere cropped heads like me don't get anywhere.' I found it incredible that a chemistry professor should speak so candidly.

'Chandrasekhar, these are trying times,' he went on. 'It's better to complete your studies here in Hyderabad and spend your life here, whether you like it or not. Students from Hyderabad State get no recognition elsewhere. There are no jobs anywhere for them. Hyderabad's merging with India is not going to help you in any way. I know how it is. Nobody outside respects a Hyderabad man. All that's not going to change overnight. Till now we had Englishmen above us; hereafter it will be Gandhi cap people. They're all the same, I tell you, as far as we are concerned; there's no escape for us.' I was afraid he might begin to cry. I came out of the room. It was quite dark outside. Professor

Tambimuthu called out from inside the room. 'That wound in your finger, did you put some iodine or something on it? It may get septic.'

5

The *Hindu* had started to reappear in Hyderabad. That evening, the attender at Somasundaram Library had dumped a bundle of about ten days' issues before Chandru and at six he had locked the library and left. When Chandru went the next day hoping to glance through the lot, he only found the day's paper on the table.

Chandru left after a cursory reading of a single day's offering. This reading room charged only four annas a month, but he was overdue by about a fortnight. So far, the attender hadn't said anything, but asking for the *Hindu* would surely draw forth a curt reminder from him. Let me see your four annas before you enter again.

Only the *Hindu*, which came from Madras, covered cricket news well. The Indian Express had flashy headlines but not enough detail. Anyway, it had also been banned here in Hyderabad, since it carried vicious attacks against the Nizam and his Government every day. When the *Hindu* was also banned, one had to be content with the three local newspapers, the *Deccan Chronicle*, the *Hyderabad Bulletin* and the *Daily News*. All three were four-page tabloids with no room for cricket. Chandru walked along Kingsway wheeling his bicycle. Yesterday's heavy downpour had cooled the city down considerably. Even otherwise, it had been quite pleasant in the last ten or fifteen days. A 'Standstill Agreement' had been reached between the Nizam and the Indian Government, and it was to be in force for a year. The Hyderabad problem had been solved, which meant some relief for the Government of India, but there were graver problems facing it: Kashmir, refugee riots in Delhi, Mahatma

Gandhi's fast. But in the midst of all this, an Indian cricket team had gone to Australia for the first time. The match in Perth was nothing to write home about. But in Adelaide, things had been different. Bradman had hit a century. Lala Amarnath had made a 144 there. And he had been stumped by Saggers off a ball by Dooland. The *Hindu* had a photograph showing Amarnath and Saggers smiling. In the next match in Melbourne Amarnath had made an unbeaten 228. India had beaten an all-Australian team in Sydney with Mankad taking eight wickets. Again, in Brisbane, Lala Amarnath made an unbeaten 172. Everyone was singing the praises of the Lala in Australia and India but little was heard of it in the Hyderabad newspapers. India, for all they cared, might have been an alien country. But there wasn't a single player from Hyderabad State on the Indian team-not Ghulam Ahmad, or E.B. Aibara, or Bhoopati, the Tamil player. One had to depend on the infrequently available *Hindu* from Madras for the cricket score. Newspapers from outside the state which had not been banned were available in Hyderabad the next day, because Madras to Hyderabad was a night and a day by train, a journey increasingly being undertaken from the Hyderabad end. Many people had left Hyderabad.

Chandru was still wheeling his bicycle. These days, it was nothing unusual for shopping centres to be deserted even during the day. Or for houses to be locked. A few hundred families from here had evacuated the town and gone to Bolaram about ten miles away. If the Indian troops stationed there were to be withdrawn according to the agreement, Bolaram would then cease to be a secure place.

There was no change in the Nizam's trips to the mosque. He still went three times every day, the police whistles stopping all traffic for him as usual. His Razakars were very much in evidence everywhere. What if the Indian Government could not counter the Nizam's machinations?

There were very few bicycles parked in front of the Arya Bhavan restaurant. It was started two years ago and had brought the real South Indian idli and coffee to Secunderabad. For just four annas you got a satisfying plate of two steamed idlis with the sambar as well as a cup of coffee. But four annas would be just enough to pay the library dues. If he had had the same four annas in British Indian coinage, it would be enough even for the matinee show of an English film. 'British Indian coinage' was not the right phrase anymore. Now it was Indian coinage. But things had not changed in the schools of Hyderabad. The sums still went something like, 'British-Indian currency Rs. 100 is the equivalent of Hyderabad halli currency Rs. 116 as 10 p. 6. How much is Rs. 30 in British Indian currency worth in Hyderabad halli?' Chandru groped in his trouser pockets to make sure that his half-anna was still there. Ever since he stopped going to college, he never seemed to have any money on him. This half-anna bit had been lying around some where and had been a chance discovery.

He had boycotted classes for quite a few days now. Mother had asked him about it when she found him at home all the time. He merely hemmed and hawed and left it at that. Before Father could take serious note of it, a big riot broke out in the city. Ten people were killed, eighty were seriously hurt, and schools and colleges were closed for a week. It was during this week that the Standstill Agreement had been signed. The implications of the agreement were not very clear. It seemed that the Indian Government and the Nizam had both agreed not to interfere in each others' affairs. But why should the Nizam interfere at all, Chandru wondered, in anything which concerned the rest of India? The man seemed to have got what he wanted, non-interference in his affairs while he ran an Islamic state in Hyderabad in perpetuity. For that matter the State had been under Muslim rule all these centuries. But the population had never been divided into warring groups till now. They had no reason to think of each other as enemies; none had lived in fear for his life or fled the place before now. But now, all at once, it had become important to find out where a person's loyalities lay. One had to prove it by joining one group and avoiding the others. The present Nizam needed slogans his forefathers had not needed for two and a half centuries: 'Long live independent Hyderabad!'

Chandru had reached the highest part of Kingsway. The street on the left would lead him to Monda and the spot where he had been attacked. If he just sat on his bicycle now and let it take him, he would roll along down the slope to the Bible House. The street to his right, leading to Ranigunj was the one he finally took past James Street. At Nallagutta, he stopped in front of a house and knocked on the door. A girl opened the door. She didn't wear a scarf over her neck. 'Is your father in?' Chandru asked. She went in without answering him, so Chandru followed her in. Her father, Syed, was resting on a cane easychair.

'Come in, young man,' he said in Tamil.

Chandru went and stood near him.

'Sit down. Would you like to have some roti?'

Chandru declined the offer. He said, 'Father's asked you to come home.'

'You must have some tea then,' said Syed and called out to a woman in the house, 'Ji, make some tea.' Then he repeated the order in Urdu, 'Chai banao.' Syed was a Tamil-speaking Muslim who had spent all his life in the southern Tamil towns of Cuddalore and Mayavaram. But now, having come to Secunderabad in his sixtieth year, he thought he should start speaking Urdu. To Chandru, however, he spoke in Tamil, using the 'da' of familiarity. 'Well then,' he said, 'why does your father want me?'

'I don't know, mama. Actually I ought to have come yesterday, but I couldn't do that until now.'

'Why didn't you come yesterday? Did you go to college?'

'No, mama, there were no classes yesterday.'

'Look at that! It's all because of the mischief-mongers, the Congresswalas. I hear they beat up college boys. Did anything like that happen to you?'

'No,' Chandru said. 'It was the police who chased us a few times. And I don't know if Father told you this. I was beaten up here in Secunderabad by two Razakars.'

'What?' cried Syed. 'The Razakars hit you? Impossible. They're such harmless people. They are having a difficult time hiding from these Congressmen. Look at the number of houses the Congress has burnt. And all the shops they've looted. And what makes my blood boil is that they've raped women, they've gone into the houses and torn all the women's veils. How can they do this when the Nizam has done so much for them and kept them in luxury? They ought to lick his feet like dogs in gratitude, really. We won't brook any more insolence from them. We'll shoot them all down. Beware! Do you know what life is like outside the Nizam's State, with no rice, no sugar, no firewood, no cloth, everything rationed? I ought to know. I've been in Madras Presidency—no proper roads, no buses, no postal facilities. You won't find buses like ours here anywhere in the world, I tell you. What else do the Congressmen want? Half the jobs in this State are held by Hindus. Tell me, what more could you want?'

'But the point is,' Chandru intervened, 'the majority of the population here is Hindu, which means you won't get anyone else for all the jobs.'

'Why not? I ask you, why not? All the beggars here are Muslims. Do you know that? So many of them starve to death. And the number of Muslim refugees who have flocked to this place would run into millions. Are you by any chance a Congresswala? Tell me. Are you? Don't go spoiling your father's name. Tell me now.'

'There are no Congressmen left in this State, mama. The party has been banned, the workers are all in jail.'

'Worthless, all of them,' fumed Syed. 'They've spoilt the place. It appears they've been released now. That was all wrong. They ought to be churned up in the oil mill. Keep off these things, my boy. Take care.'

'So when can we expect you, mama? Today?'

'Not today. I have parade today.'

'A military parade?'

'No. Just civil volunteers. Why don't you join up? I'll ask them to take you. But you won't get any musket training.'

'I'd rather not, mama.'

'All right. You don't need all this training when we're here to die for you.'

'I think I should leave now.'

'Have your tea. She's making it specially for you. Ji, is the tea ready? Tayyar ho gaya?' asked Syed, switching over to Urdu again. The tea was terrible, too weak, the like of which Chandru had never tasted before. Poor Syed didn't even know how to make a good cup of tea like the Hyderabadis, he thought.

As Chandru came out of Syed's house he met Syed's eldest son who was just coming in. The boy smiled at Chandru. He gave one the impression that he was in a perpetual dilemma. He had little of his father's passion and fervour. It could be that he hadn't been able to make any friends in this place. The father's new-found loyalties found no favour with the sons. In his native-village of Cuddalore he would not have worn such a vacuous expression. The son too would go to the parade tomorrow, the father was sure to drag him along. They would march, armed with some eighteenth-century firearms.

This Syed and Chandru's father were childhood friends, friends from their days together in their native Tamil village. Father's attitude to Syed wasn't clear, but Syed still looked upon Father as a village schoolboy from Thanjavur district. And the way he went on about the atrocities of the Congress—he was so confident that his old friend would share every opinion of his. But Syed refused to realise that it was impossible in the Secunderabad of today for two men as different as Syed and his Hindu friend to appraise things the same way. That even if they did, the consequences would be different for each of them.

Syed's son was about the same age as Nasir Ali Khan and Masood. In spite of all the disturbing things that had been happening, the two were still their natural selves. Nasir's father was a high-ranking officer in the police and belonged to one of the oldest noble families of Hyderabad. They had not betrayed any panic in public till now, though what they might do if the situation worsened further was anybody's guess. Nasir's group in college never discussed politics openly. Nor did they evince the least interest in such matters. Why, as recently as two days ago, Nasir had sent word to Chandru to come to a cricket match the following Sunday. But Chandru couldn't very well play in a match in college when he was boycotting college, could he? Sundar Singh was sure to go, however. Not unduly bothered about the present unrest in the city, Sundar Singh regarded himself as nothing but a student of an English medium college. Also a sportsman, a cricketer, a player of music on the bulbultarang, an omnivorous eater of anything served in an Irani restaurant and a church-goer on Sundays in his best suit. It would appear that he went to church more for the suit than anything else. Morris was even freer than Sundar Singh. Anglo-Indians were the least concerned about the present situation. What a hassle-free existence his would be if only he'd been a Christian or an Anglo-Indian!

Past Ranigunj and through another lane of Nallagutta, Chandru went to Narasimha Rao's house. Half a dozen houses in a row, all locked. They had been locked for some time now. The doors were covered with graffiti in chalk and charcoal—urchins' work. There were a few pictures too, a flagpole and a flag with a moon, a crescent moon. In this street which seemed to owe its allegiance to the crescent moon, the only house that was open was Narasimha Rao's. A number of families used to live in that building, but not any more. Chandru called out 'Narasimha Rao! Narasimha Rao!'

An old woman looked out. Chandru asked her in Telugu if Narasimha Rao was in. She gestured with her hand to indicate 'No'. Narasimha Rao had not been seen for a fortnight or more. He had disappeared even before the college closed after the disturbances in the city. It was he who had taken Chandru and several others to a strange place and got them to sign in blood and had ordered them not to go to college. What was to be done now? Could anything be achieved by just drifting like this, doing nothing?

'When will he come back?' Chandru asked the woman.

'I don't know.'

'He *is* here, isn't he?'

'I don't know anything,' the woman said in Telugu and went in, while Chandru continued, 'I'm his friend. We're classmates.'

Silence. A child came into view and slammed the door shut. Chandru stood there for a while and then left. From a corner of the window the curtain was lifted just a little and an eye seemed to be looking through it. Chandru caught the eye just then. It was Narasimha Rao's.

6

Colleges and schools had reopened after the disturbances. The half-yearly and selection exams were over, the Christmas holidays would soon begin. The rain had thinned and it was getting warm again. Mornings were misty. The Husain Sagar lake lay calm and the force of the wind on the Tank Bund had lessened considerably. Walking or riding along the Bund during the day was a pleasant experience in these winter months. The Nawab of Chhatari who had followed Mirza Ismail as the Chief Minister of Hyderabad had also been dismissed. During the time the Nawab of Chhatari was in office as the President of Nizam's executive council, the Razakars held a rally in front of his residence. Apparently, he didn't repeat their slogans with the necessary amount of enthusiasm, and the Razakars surrounded his house and pulled out one half of his moustache—a long and lovingly tended specimen—by its roots. When the Nawab left, the Nizam didn't even express a word of thanks to him for his services. The present incumbent, Laiq Ali, was not likely to be subjected to the same treatment as his predecessor—*he* didn't sport a moustache, for one thing. More importantly, this minister had the approval of Kasim Razvi, the leader of the Razakars. Laiq Ali had not yet turned his attention to the Tank Bund. It remained as last renovated by Sir Mirza Ismail. One had to concede this much to Mirza Ismail—he had really beautified the mile-long stretch. He didn't like the view of the lake to be blocked by a wall and so had put railings in its place. The battlement-like sit-outs on the pier had been demolished and rebuilt at the level of the pavement to enable people to walk in and have their fill of fresh air. These were small changes but they transformed the Bund into a lovelier place.

Chandru walked to the sit-out, parked his bicycle, and surveyed the scene. Far away to his left stood a building resembling the bow of a ship—the Boat Club. Behind it was the Osmania Technical Institute which had the appearance of an eighteenth-century castle with fortifications. From where he stood, Chandru could see all the sides of the lake. On the opposite side, across two miles of water were a few bungalows with the Banjara hills in the background. To his right a railway bridge spanned a canal fed by the lake. If you stood watching from here when a train entered the bridge, a clear four seconds would pass before you heard the first sounds of the train rolling past the steel girders of the bridge. What is the speed of sound? About a thousand feet per second. A four-second lag would mean some four thousand feet from the point, so the bridge must be four thousand feet away, about three quarters of a mile, that is.

Chandru stood watching the bridge, the trees and the few scattered buildings. And beyond everything, the pale blue sky hung with low clouds. In the days when he attended college regularly, he had often wished to spend a few minutes on this balcony, but had never found the time. He wasn't going to college now, though the classes went on as usual. There was time at last for a few minutes on the Tank Bund. The question was how much longer it would be possible to do things like this. Narasimha Rao had got his signature in blood—together with a number of other bloody signatures—for the Quit College Movement Nizam College was the only college in that area offering instruction in English. He had almost quit it. Now what? That was what he wanted to ask of Narasimha Rao. The man had been in his house all the time that Chandru was being fobbed off by his mother or sister with an 'I don't know anything'. Imagine placing one's trust in this man and signing in blood, blood that was thicker than water, thicker than ink no doubt, and couldn't be taken lightly.

There was not much traffic on the Tank Bund. The double-decker buses newly bought by the Nizam's government sped past smoothly. The old buses still plied, each emitting its own cloud of smoke. But with these new buses one couldn't tell that they had engines. That was perhaps the inspiration behind Syed's eloquence.

Chandru mounted his bicycle and pedalled slowly towards Hyderabad. The third hour in the morning session must be on now in college, with the lunch break to follow. Table-tennis players would have a hurried lunch and rush to the Salar Jung Hall. The table-tennis tournaments were probably on now. Chandru too could have played, if only he'd gone to college. Very few science students played table-tennis. The fun and games were all for the arts students. They had a lively time in college. At any tournament, you'd find all the history girls there. Miss Taraporewala, Miss Ananda Rao and Miss Naidu who made up the 'Diamond Set' were sure to be there. Miss Taraporewala came to college in a blue Ford Deluxe. There was only one more car of the same model in Hyderabad which was usually found parked in front of Abdul Khader and Sons. They had two big shops, one in Secunderabad, and this one in Hyderabad. They were the owners of the Grand Ice Cream Parlour near Fateh Maidan. Ice cream was served with a special kind of biscuit in the parlour. You got a feel of fibres when you bit into it, you didn't get such wafers anywhere else. An ice cream cup cost eight annas. The 'Diamond Set' ate ice cream every day. It was worth going to college, if not for anything else, just to have a look at Miss Taraporewala, her silky softness, with the veins on her neck showing as if seen through fine tissue-paper. She wore rimless glasses.

If Chandru got a chance in the table-tennis tournament, he might ask her to be his partner for the mixed doubles—she was in great demand. Chandru had never spoken to her. This benighted maths-physics-chemistry group restricted one's company to Sundar Singh, Lakshman Rao and Tambimuthu. What was one to make of Professor Tambimuthu's rash mania for Tamil songs? He ought to be content teaching chemistry. Or if he must sing, let him set Avogadro's hypothesis and the periodic table to music. By the way, what had happened to Padma Sivarao? A nice quiet girl, Padma Sivarao. She usually took four days' leave for every two days she attended class. Had she by any chance joined the Quit College Movement? Would a boycott by Padma Sivarao persuade the Nizam to bring Hyderabad into the Indian Union? At the end of the Tank Bund Chandru turned left towards Basheer Bagh. Just a ten-minute ride to college now. But what was he going to do there? Sit down in some corner and eat the puris he had brought with him? If he happened to meet someone a conversation couldn't be avoided. What if he went to class? But blood was thicker than ink. When he reached the crossroads at Fateh Maidan, Chandru didn't go to the Nizam College, he took the road that went round the tree in the direction of Nampalli. On the way to Nampalli were the Public Gardens which housed the zoo, a nice place to spend a few hours in until college was out. He could go home after that.

Amazing, wasn't it, the way he was getting sucked in deeper and deeper into these hopeless muddles with no apparent initiative, no real effort on his part? At home, the burden of the buffalo fell on him—as if it was his sole responsibility to keep it away from the church premises and the police officer's house. It had been a long time now that they had stopped playing cricket near home. Several of the boys had left Secunderabad. Those who remained could muster neither the enthusiasm nor their elders' permission to play. The playfield had now been taken over by the Muslim boys for hockey in the evenings and for martial training in the mornings when they did 'left-right' marching. Morris and Terence seemed to have grown up overnight. So it was goodbye to games like tip-cat and monkeys-on-trees. He could join the college cricket groups. Nasir Ali Khan would still let him play. But then his first day at the nets had been such a disaster. And then there was this obsession of his with girls. Yet somehow his mind didn't dwell for long on any single girl. It was Pyari Begum for a second, an Anglo-Indian girl the next. Thoughts of Nagaratnam at the Secunderabad bus-stand. The Regimental Bazaar brought memories of whats-her-name of the paraiah settlement—Pushpa. Once he had crossed over to the other side of the Tank Bund, his thoughts hovered on a Padma Sivarao or a Taraporewala or an Anandarao. He was never able to recall any of their faces clearly. This little failing of his could not have escaped them. What girl would care for a boy who failed to recognise her? He had such a hazy memory for faces. Even the Mannas girls were so aloof these days. Was that too because of the muddy state of his mind? What he needed to do was forget everything else and concentrate on his studies. But of all the lectures he had attended in the past four months, nothing, absolutely nothing, seemed to have registered in his mind. Worse, he had now set his name to a pledge that he would not attend any classes. And so here he was on his way to the zoo during class hours. Supposing he now went to the boy in whose house they had all met for the signature campaign and tried to find out...

Chandru went to the Mozamjahi Market, not a familiar locality until about two months ago. These new places and new people formed a part of his new commitments. Not that he was bound to take an active part in what was going on. He could easily turn a blind eye to the situation round him and live out his life like the rest of the family who had lived here for generations but still behaved like visitors, taking neither interest nor responsibility in the affairs of the State.

After all, problems found their own solutions in due course; family problems as well as problems of the country. Moreover, several important people were involved in the present problem of Hyderabad. There were the Razakars, Laiq Ali, Kasim Razvi, the Nizam, Jayaprakash Narayan, Vallabhbhai Patel, Jawaharlal Nehru, Swami Ramanand Tirth, Digambar Rao Bindu, Kasinath Vaidya. Theirs was the direct responsibility. They had better have all the answers. None of them, however, was going to bother about Chandru or ask him, 'Have you eaten yet?' He was just not important enough for them to bother about. Narasimha Rao and his kind were the only ones to whom Chandru mattered. But now even those people seemed to have abandoned him. A whole week's search for Narasimha Rao's group had been in vain. Everyone seemed to have vanished. It was a Hegde he wanted to meet now. A Hegde known simply as Hegde. His other name was unknown. He wouldn't tell, though Chandru had asked him. Fear of the police, perhaps. The police may take even Chandru one of these days. But he had little to confess even if they chose to tie him up and beat him. What he might reveal would be of no value to the police. All the more reason why he might be roughed up severely.

Hegde was not at home. Only an old woman. The number of old women in Hyderabad appeared to have gone up considerably.

Chandru went to the Public Gardens again. This time he went in. The gate, the fence, the buildings were all grand to look at. But the garden inside was dismal. Like the Nizam, a shrivelled up figure in crumpled clothes sitting huddled up in a corner of that huge sleek limousine. Chandru sat down on the lawn littered with garbage and dry leaves. After a while he lay down on the grass like several others there. And soon, like the others, he too went to sleep.

III

1

Chandru was standing at the gate when the astrologer came. 'Going somewhere?' he asked Chandru. It is considered a bad omen sighting a Brahmin just when one is starting out.

'No... Yes,' said Chandru.

'Anyway, come in and sit down for a while before you leave,' advised the astrologer, that being the antidote for the bad omen. Chandru stood aside to let him enter and followed him. The astrologer sat down on the long swing in the veranda. Chandru went to the kitchen and announced, 'Lord Saturn is here.'

'What? So early in the morning?' his mother wondered. 'And on an auspicious Friday too! He has come in time for a meal, that's what it is. Where's your father?'

'I don't know.'

'Must have gone to Mr Nagabhushanam's, the guard, you know.'

'Let me go and tell him then,' said Chandru.

Nagabhushanam's house was the one after Mr Mannas'. As Chandru went past Mannas' house, Morris called out, 'What, man?' Chandru nodded as if to say. 'Coming in a moment' and stepped into Nagabhushanam's. A strong smell of frying onions greeted him.

Father and Mr Nagabhushanam were sitting together deep in conversation. For the past few months, Mr Nagabhushanam had been the guard on the Secunderabad–Bezwada Express. He saw Chandru and asked him, 'What is it, master? What brings you here with bare feet and bare head?'

Chandru ignored the teasing and looked at his father. Father signalled with his eyes: 'Just sit down.' So he sat down.

Mr Nagabhushanam continued from where he had stopped. 'We get these military people only from Dornakal station. But yesterday the soldiers got in one in every compartment, right from Kazipet. Four of them got into my van. There was no room for us to stand, sit or even get to the toilet. Worse, the train was two hours late in the morning when we managed to reach there and it was already daylight by then. The train was still moving when we heard these shots, they were fired from behind some trees a furlong away. The bushes near the rail tracks have all been cleared by now as you know, but this was from the jungle beyond. I didn't know whether to stop the train or let it go on. There was this Muslim soldier in my compartment who kept asking me to stop. But I had orders not to stop anywhere in the Indo-Hyderabad border area except for police checks. I was in a real predicament there.'

'What if someone had pulled the alarm chain?' Father asked.

'Not even then. Those were our instructions. Once the border checking was done, our next stop was at Bezwada—the three halts between have all been cancelled now. Twenty-six miles more to the border, but this Muslim soldier started threatening me with his 'Stop, stop!' But the train halted anyway, even without a signal. I peeped out and knew why. Two soldiers had jumped down from the engine.'

'What then? What happened?'

'All the Nizam's soldiers jumped off the train, and some hefty Razakars with them. They screamed and shouted and took off in a mad run towards the shots.'

'Didn't the communists fire at the soldiers?'

'No,' said Nagabhushanam. 'Surprising, isn't it? I really don't know why they didn't shoot. Perhaps the sight of the army had put some fear into them. Anyway, it was these soldiers and Razakars who went on a rampage and ten minutes later came back with a few Lambadi tribals, two men and three women. And then—the whole thing is just too terrible for words.'

'Were they beaten up?'

'Beaten is not the word for it. They tore the men to pieces, hitting and spearing them with sticks and guns, rolling and kicking them as they died. The women went on screaming at the sight and they were also beaten up. And then, ... in front of all of us... they tore off their clothes.'

'What!'

'Yes. The drawstrings of their skirts were not easy to untie. They just cut them with their knives. Then they started pawing at them and dragging them around, all naked and wounded... they kept driving them away but the poor women came back wailing to their men who now lay dead. It was unbearable... ghastly.'

Mr Nagabhushanam fell silent and sat staring ahead in a shocked daze. Father too sat petrified. And if Chandru was able to withstand the shock better, it was only because this was by no means the first time he was hearing about such happenings. For some time now, the Indo-Hyderabad border, especially the district of Warangal had been reeling under the combined assault of Hyderabad's police and military forces. As part of their fight against communist guerillas, the land on either side of the railway tracks had been cleared of all cover for miles. Few communists were caught by these measures but the Lambadi tribes became the unfortunate victims. Lambadi women wore elaborately embroidered and mirror-studded skirts and blouses. Once worn, these clothes were not supposed to be changed at all till the funeral fire burnt them to ashes along with their bodies. A people with these customs and beliefs were now fleeing for their lives because of the Razakars and the Nizam's army. In normal times, these tribals were considered beneath notice and they generally went through life wallowing it together in subhuman conditions. But when they started helping the communists, they fell upon evil days. Saturn's bane had caught up with them too!

Chandru said softly to his father: 'The astrologer has come.'

'Wait a minute,' said Father.

The tension caused by the reminiscences eased a bit and Mr Nagabhushanam asked Father, 'Shall I come to the office today?'

'Why? Have you any special work there?'

'I've applied for a pass.'

'A pass for—?'

'My family of course.'

'To go where?'

'Madras.'

'You mean you've already got the police permit?'

'Can't I do without it?'

'Yes if you want to travel within Hyderabad State. Elsewhere no railway tickets or passes are issued without the police permit. You must know all that yourself.'

Mr Nagabhushanam was silent. The presence of four strong men in his house—his nephew, his two grown-up sons and himself—did not seem to reassure him much. He was bent on sending everyone out of Hyderabad. 'Still, there's no harm trying,' he insisted.

'Well, I'll have a look at your application,' Father said. 'But even the English officers are a bit careful in these matters. The permit can be had from the Secunderabad court offices. You know the place, near the YMCA on Alexandra Road, not too far, you can go there yourself and collect it.'

'Let me see. What about you? Aren't you sending your family out?'

'Where does one send them?' Father said. 'Madurai is a possibility, my sister lives there. But with just three months to go for the children's annual exams... I may send them after the exams.'

'You don't expect the exams to be held this year do you? Schools lost many working days because of the riots. In colleges I understand the classes are half empty.'

Chandru felt unnerved. He had been avoiding all adults just because questions about college might come up.

'Anyway, let's wait and see.' Chandru's father got up. 'See you then.'

'Good, master. I'll come to your office in the afternoon. Please try to issue that pass for me.'

'I'll try my best,' said Father. 'By the way, what about the other thing I asked you?'

'Sorry. I couldn't bring any this time. Next time, I'll try to bring at least ten seers.'

'But there's no rice at home; not a grain, friend.'

'I'll try next time, for sure. Please do something about my pass.'

Chandru followed his father out. It was getting late for Father. Just enough time to change into a formal dhoti, coat and cap and start for work. He could have his meal only at one in the afternoon when he came back from the office.

The astrologer stood when he saw Father. 'Oh, welcome. When did you come?' said Father.

'Sometime ago,' the astrologer said. 'I thought your son told you?'

'Have you had your bath yet?' asked Father.

'Yes. An early bath.'

'Then you can have something to eat. I'm late for the office. I'll see you in the afternoon.'

'It's not good,' the astrologer said, 'to go out without eating on an auspicious day like today, a Friday of the Tai month.'

'But I had to see someone about getting some rice,' said Father. 'It's all right. Go ahead and eat. I'll see you in the afternoon.'

Father hurried off to work and Chandru and the astrologer sat down to eat. Mother first served them cooked greens on their banana leaves and asked the astrologer if he minded eating maize rotis.

'Don't bother to ask,' said the astrologer. 'It's the same thing in every house these days.'

'The ration rice is hardly enough for two days,' Mother said. 'And then it's a *red* variety. And now for the past two weeks there's been no sugar at all.'

'It seems there's a famine all over the country. My nephew came over from Tiruvarur the day before yesterday. It appears things are no better there, to go by what he says.'

'But one needn't fear for one's life and limb in those places, that's something,' said Mother.

Chandru broke off a piece of the maize roti, scooped up a little of the cooked greens with it and ate it. In this princely state of the Nizam, the only things available in plenty these days were greens, maize and peanut oil.

Whatever rice was available did not reach the ration shop. Wheat was being supplied for some time, but had been stopped now. Sugar may or may not be given once a month. Their coffee was sweetened with rock sugar now. As long as Indian troops were stationed at Bolaram, it was possible to get some sugar from the military quota through some acquaintance in the army. It was now two months since the army had left. True, K.M. Munshi, the Indian representative, was there. He had a secretary who was a distant relative of Father's but how was one to ask him for sugar? By the way, this was the same K.M. Munshi, the astute lawyer who had defended the Tamil actors M.K. Tyagaraja Bhagavatar and N.S. Krishnan in the Lakshmikanthan murder case.

He was not able to do much for them, though. It was only after the appeal went to London that the two were finally released. So here was K.M. Munshi, now in the Nizam's State. He had been successful in preventing a confrontation between India and Hyderabad. But would he be able to save the Lambadis?

Mother served them a little rice, not enough really, but she spooned out generous quantities of curd to mix it with. When they had eaten and gone to wash their hands, the astrologer asked Chandru, 'Aren't you going to college?'

Chandru pretended not to have heard the question and offered him water from the bucket to wash. But the man didn't give up: 'You haven't gone to college today.'

'No.'

'Is it still closed?'

'No.'

'Reopened?'

'Yes.'

'Then why haven't you gone?'

'I don't have any class today.'

'Is that possible?'

'Hm.'

Mother heard everything but desisted from intervening. Chandru left the astrologer and went to the buffalo-shed. The buffalo nodded a welcome. Chandru scratched its ear. The animal's enjoyment was evident in the appreciative quiver that passed through its frame. Chandru patted its back. The poor animal hadn't had a full feed for two days now. The store of dry grass had all been used up. For the past ten days, Chandru had been going to Monda every evening to fetch some grass for it on his bicycle. But you can't load much grass on a bicycle. Grass carts rarely came to Lancer Barracks these days. A carter did come the week before, but his price was too high and they had bought only a little. Thank heaven for the cotton seed and oil cake which were still available. But too much oilcake gave the buffalo diarrhea. Anyway oilcake did not satisfy it. It had to have grass.

Chandru went out through the back door and looked at the expanse of rough country that lay beyond the second line of Lancer Barracks and the quiet church and the bungalows, police officer Kasim's bungalow among them. Months had gone by since he went there last. Nobody came now to graze the buffalo. She stayed tied up all the time. If let loose now, she would take off at once and wouldn't stop till she reached the police officer's house. His garden was indeed the most luxuriant in the vicinity.

Chandru walked in the direction of the military cemetery. It was quite far but appeared rather near. Even the gate of the cemetery couldn't be opened any more, the whole place was overrun with weed and shrub. Here a few people long dead had become a part of this earth. Even the

British had died. Even the British had left India. And now it was time for Hindus to leave Hyderabad. The British had no problem leaving India, but where could these people go? What would it be like if all the Hindus of Hyderabad went to India and all the Muslims of India came over to Hyderabad? What about the Anglo-Indians and Parsis? If the whole of Lancer Barracks was occupied only by Muslims, some sort of collective cooking would be possible in huge aluminium cauldrons. They could supplement it with the food made by the refugees. Only, the whole neighbourhood would suffocate with the stink. How could they eat meat when it smelt so foul? Mercilessly they killed all those trembling twitching goats here to celebrate Bakrid! Thanks to the Muslim household next door, he did know such details. Otherwise, all he would have known would be Nasir's cricket and Masood's silk sherwani. The Nizam who looked like dried and salted okra and the old women of Hyderabad who all looked like him. Then Pyari Begum, and that vision just descended from the clouds, Nasir's sister, with the tracery of blue-green veins on her fair neck, just like Nargis Taraporewala. Nargis too was beautiful, but her eyes spoke of experience. Somehow such eyes diminished beauty.

As he stood out in the open, Chandru suppressed a sigh. He found it possible to control himself these days even when a weeping fit seemed imminent. How long was he going to stay at home? The only times he went out these days was when he went to shop for vegetables once every three or four days or when he got the maize ground in the mill or fetched some grass for the buffalo. He had given up college altogether. Perhaps his name was off the rolls by now. Getting readmitted was not much of a problem in the colleges here, but a year would be lost, this if the examinations did take place this time.

A fit of nostalgia seized him. Things connected with the college, plain ordinary things had acquired excitement now that he had ceased going there—the gate of the college, the peepal tree at the intersection of the three roads, the Salar

Jung Hall, the science block, the playfields, the lecture halls of the Arts Section, that fan with the missing blade in one of them. He had once aimed a notebook at it while it was whirling at full speed. Fortunately, there was no one else present to see the blade break off. These inanimate things apart, there were many living beings, humans he missed. He missed the known, familiar faces. He longed to see Miss Taraporewala. He had little in common with her. She wasn't of his caste or community, and she couldn't speak a word of Tamil, try as hard as she might. She wouldn't like any of his favourite food, just as he wouldn't like any of hers, Abdul Khadar Ice Cream being the sole exception. Yet, his heart yearned for a look at her face.

Someone seemed to be calling him from home. He went in by the backyard door. Both his sisters had come home for lunch. The astrologer was asleep on the long plank of the swing.

'Chandru get some chilli ground for me, will you?' said Mother.

'Have you dried the pods well?'

'As dry as is possible in these winter days. Here, see for yourself.'

Chandru took a dried pod of red pepper and crushed it between his fingers. It felt limp. 'No, this won't do,' he said. 'They'll refuse to grind it; it's a waste going all the way.'

'But there's not a pinch of powder left.'

'Let me pound some in the mortar for you, then.'

Mother wiped the mortar clean and Chandru sat down before it, iron pestle in hand. Mother filled the bowl of the mortar with the chilli and Chandru brought the pestle down on it with a loud thud. That was when he heard the front gate being opened. He could see it from where he sat—when Father left in the morning he had forgotten that Father had not eaten before he left for office and he would be home for lunch. Impossible to escape him now, the nuisance of it. Try as he might to avoid his father, he always seemed to slip somewhere and find himself trapped. But then was there anything wrong with an eldest son pounding chilli at home? Nothing. Why was it an unbearable embarrasment before Father now? But it was Father himself who seemed to find the situation awkward. It was rather difficult to understand him. He had hardly exchanged a dozen words with Chandru in the last two months. Today he did speak to him but it was just a few words. It looked as if it was Father who was trying to avoid him.

The astrologer was still asleep. Father had a leisurely meal. Mother served him only one maize roti. He soaked it in buttermilk and ate it.

Chandru's nose began to burn. He must have touched it after touching the chilli. By now the pods had been crushed to tiny pieces, but the seeds still remained whole. It seemed impossible to pound any further. Whenever his pestle missed the stuff at the bottom and struck the side of the mortar, a head-splitting 'klong!' reverberated through the house. But the astrologer slept on.

After she had served Father, Mother came and stirred the contents of the mortar with an iron ladle. Then she began to sift the powder. There were more rough pieces left on the sieve than powder under it.

Then Father left for the office again and Mother began to make maize rotis for the next meal. She found it difficult to knead and spread the dough, and she called Chandru. He went to help her without a word of protest.

The astrologer woke up at last just as Chandru's brother Pitchumani returned from school. A few minutes later the girls were also back. Mother called them in turn to come and eat their tiffin. But there were no takers for the maize rotis except the astrologer and Chandru. It was only when Father came back from the office and sat down with the astrologer with a sheaf of horoscopes that the latter's visit began to take on some significance. They discussed each of their horoscopes. The astrologer had read these times without number and by now surely knew the past, present and future of everyone in the family. Bless the man, had it not been for his diagnosis of the malign influence of the seven-and-a-half-years' Saturn on Chandru, his parents, like any other parents would have been quite harsh with him at this time, naturally.

Night had fallen when all of them except Pitchumani left for the temple near the railway station. It couldn't have been less than a mile away. The astrologer also came along, but disappeared somewhere when they were nearing the temple. There were very few people in the temple. Since there was a mosque nearby, people were always very cautious in their worship. Bells were never rung loud. There was no singing or playing of instruments. But caution had reached egregious proportions now. The sacred Ashtotra chants in praise of Ganesha had now become intimate whispers.

They returned from the temple in their usual procession—Father first, followed by Chandru, then the two girls, with the rear brought up at a considerable distance by Mother. They had come just half a furlong when a friend of Father's accosted him, asked him something and then went away. Father looked agitated. Someone in coat and cap was approaching them from the opposite direction, and Father asked him 'Is it true? Has Gandhi been shot?' Chandru went and stood by his father. The stranger replied in anger: 'He's been dead these two hours, and here you go wondering if he was really shot.'

2

The family procession lost its rhythm. Father walked a bit faster than usual. Mother and the girls also hurried, sensing the urgency. Chandru kept ahead of them all, in a half-run, and turned only once to look at them.

Charles Street rose and fell past Keyes High School, cut through Oxford Street, rose again and disappeared past the limit of Maredpalli. The street wore a deserted look, all three quarters of a mile of it, flanked on either side by the walled-in buildings which lay far in and were lost in the darkness.

Within Lancer Barracks, the houses had very dim lights, a measure of economy, perhaps also a ruse to ensure that the place drew no attention. There was safety in going through life unnoticed. But strangely nobody was even listening to the radio today.

Chandru saw Morris at the banyan tree. It had been a while since they had exchanged words. Morris too was getting to be an adult. He too must have been burdened with anxiety about his future. But now he saw Chandru and said, 'Hello.'

'Any news?' asked Chandru.

'What about?'

'Gandhi.'

'Gandhi who?'

'Mahatma Gandhi.'

'Oh,' said Morris. 'What about him?'

'I heard he's been shot dead.'

'Really?'

Morris lifted his arms and caught at a hanging root of the banyan. He would start swinging soon, even in this dark night, thought Chandru and asked him, 'Don't you know anything?'

'No,' said Morris and began to swing on an aerial root just as Chandru had expected.

Chandru let him swing and went home. He remembered about the keys only when he reached there. It was always Mother who had the keys and whoever reached home earlier had to wait for her. Chandru didn't want to wait. He ran back the way he came. A surprised Morris asked him, 'What man?' Chandru hurried off without stopping to answer him. At the top of the street he met Father.

'Where are you off to again?' he asked.

'To get the key.'

'Why? Isn't Pitchumani at home?'

Chandru ran back home. He had forgotten that they hadn't locked the house today because his brother had stayed back. Morris again, on the way. But he didn't say anything to Chandru this time. When he reached home Chandru asked his brother, 'Why're you sitting in the dark? Can't you put the lights on?'

Pitchumani didn't reply. When Chandru ran to the radio and switched it on, he came and stood by him and watched. The radio usually needed a minute to warm up. But twice the time passed and no sounds were heard. '*Ai,* why don't you put the light on?' he asked his brother and flicked a switch on himself. A half-hearted yellow gleam appeared in the bulb.

'Why is it so dim?' he asked his brother. This was the first time in four or five months that Chandru was speaking to him.

'How do I know?' came his brother's reply.

Chandru came out and peeped into their neighbour Mr Kasim's house. Mr Kasim's radio was never silent at eight in the evening. But today his house was quiet. The lights too were dim.

Father, Mother and the others reached the house. 'Why don't you switch on the radio?' asked Mother. Father must have told her about Gandhi. 'The radio isn't working,' said Chandru. Mother went in to look for the hurricane lantern.

Chandru fumbled among the contents of the drawer for the few coins he kept there, about four annas. He took the money and went out. Mother was discussing something with Father, she'd forgotten all about dinner. Gandhiji's death had affected her schedule as well.

For the first time Chandru noticed that no radios or electric lights were on in the whole of Lancer Barracks. Oil lamps were lit, but they only served to exaggerate the darkness beneath the twenty-foot-high roof. When he walked past Morris' house, Mr Mannas' voice called out, 'You, man? So Gandhi's dead?'

'Who told you, sir?' asked Chandru.

'My son.'

'Who? Terence?'

'No, Morris.'

Without a word, Chandru hurried away. There were four or five persons with Morris under the banyan now. Without turning to look at them, Chandru went on to the street. There was no one on the street. He walked towards the clock tower. Oxford street too would be empty, with its long high walls on either side, protecting the houses tucked in somewhere in the interior. The spacious grounds of these houses posed a maintenance problem and were left to go to seed, full of grass and snakes. He had seen snakes lying on the road crushed by the wheels of passing cars and motorcycles. It was mid-winter now and snakes were not seen at night during the cold months. Well, if they did choose to come out now, running away was all he could do.

Even without sighting any snake, Chandru began to run, sandals flapping against heels—*padak, padak, padak.* Good in a way, he thought. Any stray snake inclined to come out off-season could take warning from the noise and hide itself.

A few lights were on and some people were standing near the clock tower. The noise of the electric motors of the Allauddin Ice Factory was audible. Gossip had it that the Allauddin family were not in the good books of the Nizam and that he had financed another Allauddin, a relative of this Allauddin, to start a factory called 'G. Allauddin Ice-fruit Factory.' There was a demand for ice cream and ice fruit even in winter! With so much electricity being consumed, this place was sure to have a radio. Could he go in and find out about Gandhiji? Kingsway was also deserted. That was unusual on a Friday, because on Fridays the shops were generally open till 9.30 at night. Perhaps some news could be had from a cinema hall. Evening papers like the *Hyderabad Bulletin* might carry the news. Why, he could have bought a copy by now if only he'd thought of going to the railway station. What had made him come this way to the clock tower? He ought to have asked that angry man on the road for more details, the one who said Gandhi had been dead for two hours. But how could he when Father was there? Father could have asked him but didn't. Why? Did he by any chance dislike Gandhi? Could anyone dislike Gandhi? Except the person who shot him? Who was he? A Muslim?

Chandru felt a sudden surge of heat course through his veins. A Muslim? If he did turn out to be a Muslim, he would kill ten Muslims with his own hands. A hundred perhaps. As many as possible. Including the Nizam and Kasim Razvi. As if the Muslims would oblige him and stand in a row, necks all stretched to be hacked down. Those who did stand these days, offering their necks, were all Hindus. And also those poor Lambadis. By the way, were the Lambadis Hindus or Muslims?

Chandru went to the Minerva Hall. The evening show seemed to have ended and the crowd had left. The betelnut stall was open, with a boy keeping shop. Chandru asked him in Telugu, 'Know anything about Gandhiji?'

'Yes sir. A madman has killed him.'

'How do you know?'

'We heard it on the radio. By 7.30 the news had spread and all shops downed their shutters here and in Kingsway.'

'But we around the railway station know absolutely nothing about it.'

'Well, the whole city knows.'

Not the whole of it, thought Chandru. Or perhaps Lancer Barracks was not part of the city. With no power, even radios denied, Lancer Barracks was not the least concerned about this soul, Gandhi. And in any case, all those Anglo-Indians and Muslim Razakars of Lancer Barracks had never at any time considered Gandhi. No. Never. Gandhi and all that was none of their business. Chandru felt bitter.

Was Gandhi really dead? Oh no! He had always said he would live to be a hundred and twenty-five. This must be just a rumour. The news appeared to have come over the radio. But what if the radio had lied? Like in those war days? When the British claimed the Germans lied and the Japs said the British lied? This must surely be a lie. How could Gandhi die? Think of all those fasts he had been through. The twenty-one-day fast, with those constant reports of 'He's dying... dying... dying...' But he had survived.

Chandru went as far as the Tivoli Cinema in search of a newspaper. The owners of the cinema were also the proprietors of the *Hyderabad Bulletin. So* this was the one place where the paper should be available. Boys with bundles of the paper were always seen hawking it in Tivoli. But Chandru had seen them only in the afternoons and evenings. It was rather foolish to expect them to hawk newspapers at this time of night when they had wound up for the day.

That night's show had been cancelled at the Tivoli. All the betelnut stalls and stores attached to the cinema had also been closed. Only the manager's room was open. Chandru went and stood at the door. The man inside asked, 'Who's that?'

'I'd like to get a copy of the *Bulletin,* please,' said Chandru.

'But we're closed.' When Chandru made to go, he said, 'Take my copy if you like'. Then he took out the newspaper from the drawer and handed it to Chandru. Chandru turned the pages hurriedly. The single sheet of paper was folded in four. News items and advertisements: 'G. Ramachari Appointed to Hyderabad's Council.' That would mean that this Hindu would have to serve under the fanatic Muslim Chief Minister, Laiq Ali. Then there had been another rally by the Ittihad-ul-Muslimin, the organisation of Kasim Razvi. 'Atrocities of the Indian Government: Plot to Starve and Subdue the Twenty Million People of Hyderabad!' proclaimed the paper and went on: 'The Indian Government Denies Hyderabad Essential Commodities—Petrol, Diesel, Medicines, Food, Manufactured Goods, Cars, Lorries, Chlorine Needed for Purifying Water.'

Then an outburst of Razakar rhetoric—'Is Hyderabad a leasehold of the Indian Government? It is a quirk of history that the jailbirds of yesterday should now be oppressing princes of the old lineage. Here in Hyderabad we have a three-centuries old royal house blessed by Allah. A line of seven generations of kings. But now, the days of the Indian blackguards are numbered. The foam-topped waves of the Bay of Bengal shall soon wash the feet of our Rustom-i-Dewan, Arastu-i-zamon, Lt. General, Muzaffar-al-Mulk, Wal-Mumaik, Fateh Jung Sippah Salar Mir Usman Ali Khan Bahadur Nizam-ul-Mulk, Asaf Jah. The waters of the Arabian Sea shall wet the beautiful sandals of the Nizam, the faithful ally of the British Government. The sacred Asaf Jahi flag shall fly over the Red Fort at Delhi.'

Chandru scanned every page and every inch of the *Bulletin* but there was nothing about Gandhi. So Gandhi was not dead then.

'Why are you giving the papers back? Don't you want them?'

'It was just that somebody began a rumour that Gandhi is dead. I thought I should check.'

'That's no rumour, boy. It's true. That's why we've cancelled tonight's show.'

'God! It's true, then!'

'Yes my boy, true, sadly true.'

'But there's nothing in the papers.'

'This issue was printed at four.'

'Not a single word in it.'

'He was not dead then,' he said with grief in his voice, and turned the knobs of a radio that was lying in a corner. It did not look like a radio at all from where Chandru stood. As the man turned its knobs, it presented a simulation of mustard seeds spluttering in hot oil. The man was about to switch it off when suddenly he sat up straight and alert, and fine-tuned the set. He said 'Listen. That's Pandit Nehru.' The voice spoke in English.

'The light has gone out of our lives and there is darkness everywhere. The light has gone out, I said, and yet I was wrong. For the light that shone in this country was no ordinary light. The light that has illumined this country for these many, many years will illumine this country for many more years, and a thousand years later that light will be seen in this country and the world will see it and it will give solace to innumerable hearts. For that light represented something more than the immediate present, it represented the living, the eternal truths.'

The radio went on but Chandru came out of the room. A cinema hall in a remote corner of the town had killed Gandhi. Gandhi was really and truly dead. The darkness of the January night seemed intensified by the trees on the road. There was darkness everywhere. The light had gone. It was no ordinary light. And yet at that time his mind had had room only for the details of the physical reality. There was nothing left for him to do now but to go back home—a two-and-a-half-mile walk from Tivoli. It was the Cantonment area where until recently military trucks hurtled up and down like demons. The army had gone away now, though ghosts of it probably hovered over the cemetery on the parade grounds. There had to be quite a few of the Christian variety. Even Tivoli Cinema was supposed to have its resident ghost. If all who died became ghosts could Gandhi also have become one? Could he at least see Gandhi's ghost?

He had never seen Gandhi. The names of all those places Gandhi had visited, all the places he had stayed in, sounded like places in some imaginary world: Wardha, Yeravda Prison, Sevagram, Sabarmati, Noakhali, Hindi Prachar Sabha of Madras.

Ah, the Hindi Prachar Sabha in Madras. Gandhi had come down to Madras, to visit this organisation, but never Hyderabad State. He had visited every part of India but not Secunderabad. Was it that the people here had no love for him? No *need* of him?

'Gandhi! Gandhi!' Chandru screamed the name as he ran. His voice stilled the insects of the night for a moment. From somewhere on the darkened branches of a tree a bird cried back in distress. Chandru left the road and ran across the parade grounds wailing, 'Gandhi...! Gandhi...!' The grounds were large—even hundreds of military trucks and troops together would hardly cover a small part of it. The vast barren land had tree-lined roads on all sides, but the trees had now merged with the darkness of the night and were invisible. The vast expanse of the sky was sprinkled with tiny stars. A small bush tripped him up and Chandru fell flat on his face. The ground had been flattened hard with red earth, the colour of which was not distinguishable at night but there were many big and small stones with edges sharp enough to hurt. He was hurt badly. Blood trickled from his head down to his lips. Chandru sat up and began to pound and kick and pummel the earth. 'You're dead now, dead, dead, *dead.*'

Then he stood up. He had hurt his hands and legs as well. He began to run again, in another direction, towards the cemetery. He tripped and fell again. 'I haven't seen you even once!' He beat the ground again and again, raised his voice as much as he could and cried, 'Oh Gandhi! Gandhi!' He looked all round as if expecting Gandhi to materialise. He was amazed at his own frenzy.

He then began to scratch the ground with his fingernails. It was hardened earth and didn't yield much—a handful of dust was all he could collect. He threw it up skywards. Then he got up again and dashed forward into another frantic, aimless run. When he fell down again, he began to bang his head on the ground.

A car zoomed past on the road by the race course. It must have been a good half-mile away, but Chandru began to race towards it, running for all he was worth. But it was gone. Then he fell again. His whole body was burning though he felt the cold mist through his torn clothes. He tore them some more. He tripped near a heap of gravel meant for some construction work on the site and began to throw the stones about, until he sprained his right shoulder. The last effort to fling a stone made him cry out in pain. 'Amma!'

By now his breath was like bellows, his whole body aching and sore but the frenzy in him hadn't drained. The pain that lingered was that of being tricked, cheated, betrayed. Looking at the sky, he hurled a stone at it, this time with his left hand. A short parabola, followed by a plop. That was all. The sky looked just as rt had always looked and the stars twinkled as they had always twinkled, winking among themselves like naughty children.

As he lay flat on the ground, exhausted, the night seemed to take on different hues. A viscous layer of darkness floated above the air. He shot out his hands, slamming them on the ground. Then he waved them in a wilder arc. He realised he was lying on a cricket pitch. Perhaps a pitch he himself had played cricket on. Thoughts of home came to him. Would the lights be on now? Or would everyone still be groping about in the dark?

Maybe they were asleep by now. No they would all be waiting for him, awake. Very confused about news of Gandhi, not knowing what really happened. They were probably crying. None of them would have the heart to eat. Dinner would be left untouched in the kitchens, for rats and roaches to have their fill. And the poor buffalo would be lowing away neglected.

Lying in the open in absolute solitude was soothing. Wasn't it? But was it? Wasn't it? One thing was certain now, he had been betrayed, betrayed even by Gandhi.

Anger and sorrow welled up, the wilderness become unbearable, and he began to run. All the pictures he had ever seen of Gandhi floated before him. Once there had been a photograph of Gandhi—a large one—stuck on the front of a decorated railway engine. That had been his last ever glimpse, his last ever contact with Gandhi. That had been the locomotive of the train in which Gandhi had toured South India. A locomotive just as black as the darkness now. And now here he was, panting and puffing like a locomotive. He stopped suddenly, screamed, and once again slumped to the ground, sobbing.

3

Nagaratnam had come home. Though delayed by a month, the university examinations had somehow been conducted. Only half the college students had paid their examination fees, and only half of those who had paid up had sat for the exams and God knew how many would get through. But Nagaratnam had done well. Her family had decided to leave Secunderabad. Her father had grown a moustache and beard under the pretext of being ill. That had taken care of the medical certificate needed for two months' leave. He had also managed a police permit to leave the State. It only remained now for the Twelve Down to take them up to Kazipet Junction the following Saturday. They'd reach Kazipet at night and wait there for four hours until the Grand Trunk Express came in and their carriages were attached to it. Anyhow, that was how it usually was. The hope was that things would remain the same this whole week.

After that, it would be Bezwada at eight-thirty in the morning and Madras in the evening. That was freedom. If things improved in Hyderabad, they might come back. Otherwise, they'd settle down somewhere else. There were many colleges in Madras Presidency. 'Only my father will have to come back here,' Nagaratnam said. 'It's two years to his retirement. I came to say goodbye to all of you. Chandru, will you remember me? Why, what's happened to your face? You look awful. Will you write to me? I'll write to all of you.'

Chandru stood gazing at Nagaratnam's face. It had become customary with him to let those who spoke to him go on while he continued to watch their faces. It had been a long time since he had seen Nagaratnam at close quarters. When you saw a girl in a crowd, in a public place, you had an impression of her which stayed with you. Seen as close as this, Nagaratnam did not conform to his image of her at all. She was altogether too grown up and too dark. Her face was not all that silken and smooth—did she really have so many warts and blemishes? A fine growth of hair covered her forehead and cheeks so that her hair went beyond her hairline, much like the way she herself was now going to step beyond the limits of Hyderabad.

'Why don't you say something?' Nagaratnam said, flashing an affectionate smile at him.

'Just thinking of something.'

'You're not listening to me, of course.'

'I *am* listening.'

'Impossible, you didn't hear a word of what I said, I'm sure.'

'Shall I repeat everything you said?'

'Oh forget it.'

For a while neither spoke. Then Nagaratnam said: 'In a way, I'm glad to leave this place. But also afraid. Our relatives who stay in so many places are all so different from us. To think I must go and live among them—it's really frightening... But there you go drifting into your own thoughts again.'

'Shall I say something?'

'What?'

'What's been on my mind.'

Nagaratnam seemed to shrink a little. Chandru could see that her instinctive wariness didn't allow her to let him go on. Never before had she spoken to him for any length of time. She had always treated him like a child, patronisingly. What was more, she could communicate that that was all he was to her without her so much as moving a muscle on her face, or flicking an eyelid. All the while, she knew quite well that Chandru waited at all sorts of places just to catch a glimpse of her. But today, there was a new-found security in her imminent departure. She could be generous with him and talk to him. Why, it was only two months ago that there was a new rumour about her, that she had gone missing for two days. That a girl with such an experience behind her could say she was afraid...

'Goodbye then,' she said and floated out, leaving Chandru a little dazed. She had walked in when least expected, spent an incredible ten minutes with him and walked out, leaving him no chance to prove the relationship. Just for a while she seemed so intimate and the next moment she was gone.

I have no need for such girls, thought Chandru. I'm finished with them. Six months ago, if she'd spoken to me, it would have made my day. Women cannot rouse me any more. Nagaratnam was still in the house, taking leave of everyone. Chandru still had a chance to draw attention and he might just... After all, she was going to leave them for ever... But no, he didn't make the effort.

The gulmohar tree in their garden was ablaze with red flowers. Great regulars for observing seasonal rhythms, these trees never let down the month of May. The rains of Hyderabad were as regular too. Come 6th or 7th June and you found the first rains knocking at the door. Not heavy rains, of course. If Hyderabad ever got real rains, you wouldn't find people subsisting on maize and custard apple, would you?

Quite unlike the radiant-looking gulmohar, the peepal, margosa and banyan looked withered. The grass on the ground had shrivelled to pale stumps. Thorny bushes had survived. There was even a yellow flower among the thorns. A mass of red flowers on the tree above, and on the ground, as far as the eye could see, a single yellow flower. These days, the jars and tins in the kitchen were all empty. One could barely manage to scrape together a little grain from the bottoms of the tins. Vegetables were available but little else for cooking—no salt, no chilli. Even groundnut oil had become a scarce item because buses had now switched over from diesel to groundnut oil. The fares had been doubled to make up for the cost. There was one consolation in all this—there might be little cooking worth the name going on in your own kitchen, but you had only to go out into the streets to get the smell of a feast. Half the oil in the buses went up in smoke. But the smoke-smothered city was also enveloped in the smell of fritters—bajji, vadai, omapodi, karaboondi.

The Nagpur refugees were still hawking these snacks and a lot of restaurants—Hindu as well as Muslim—bought up all they made. After all, everyone had to eat. No distinctions there. Father was going through a bad time in his office. A Muslim had taken charge. He spoke only Urdu and ran the office in Urdu. A host of others like him had been inducted into the Railway Department, which untill now was the preserve of the British, Anglo-Indians, and the Tamil and Telugu speaking peoples. It had now been taken over by the Nizam. The new recruits were largely from Maharashtra and Bihar. Each group spoke its own brand of Urdu. Father said they had problems following each other's Urdu.

Father was also afraid, afraid of some indistinguishable menace. A policeman had snatched away his walking stick and taken him to the police station the other day for carrying a dangerous weapon. The sub-inspector warned him and let him off, but didn't return the stick. There were other walking sticks at home but Father gave up carrying a stick. It was sad to see him go out without his stick.

He then stopped going out at all, almost. Everybody at home had stopped going out too. People seldom ventured out in the whole town, for that matter. Nagaratnam had come out by herself, brave girl. Her people at home may not have known. The times were such that formal leave-taking before one went out had to be given up.

Mr Kasim next door was shouting for Father. Chandru peeped out and said, 'Father hasn't returned from the office yet.'

'There's no water in our tap,' Kasim shouted. 'You've tampered with something, haven't you?'

In normal times one never heard Kasim's voice, and his radio could be mistaken for being the sole occupant of his house. But for some days now he had been shouting at Chandru's father, intimidating him.

'But we've done nothing,' Chandru said. 'Actually, we haven't been getting water either.'

'You want me to believe that? When I can hear the water all the time? What are you people up to?'

'But we haven't done anything at all—' Before Chandru could finish Kasim had jumped over the wall that separated the front-yards of their two houses. He pushed Chandru aside and went into the house in his slippers. Chandru followed him.

Hurrying past the prayer room and kitchen, Kasim reached the tap in the backyard. Every two adjacent houses in Lancer Barracks shared a connection from the water mains. The supply was very poor these days. Kasim went to the tap and said, 'See?'

Chandran didn't find anything wrong with it. His mother peeped out timidly from the kitchen.

'You seem to think you can leave your tap open all the time, don't you?' Kasim closed the tap, screwing it tight with all his strength, then looked round the backyard. His eyes fell on the buffalo's trough.

'Look at *that!*' he cried. 'Wasting water on animals when we don't have a drop for humans. Listen. This creature should leave the place by nightfall today.'

Mother showed a bit of herself and said placatingly in Tamil, 'It's mostly swill from the kitchen that we feed it, not fresh water ever.'

Kasim turned upon her, 'You people seem to think you own this place! These are railway quarters. How dare you keep a buffalo here? If I reported it, you would be thrown out with all your pots and pans in two days. So look out.'

As he was leaving, Kasim said to Chandru, 'When your father comes, ask him to see me.' The buffalo grunted just then. Kasim went in again, gave it a vicious kick and came out. When he had gone, Chandran went to bolt the front door shut. Pyari Begum, who was standing in Kasim's garden, gave him a secret smile. Perhaps she had no idea of what her father had done just now. Kasim had never behaved that way at any time in the past. Chandru bent his head and closed the door. What had happened was not unusual. There had always been arguments with maids, milkmen, sweepers, carpenters, tailors, tongawalas. They had even quarrelled with Kasim's family several years ago. That sobriquet for Pyari Begum as a special kind of sow dated from one of those fights. But Kasim had never involved himself in any of these neighbourly fracases. Now he was spoiling for a fight.

Mother and daughters sat in a huddle. When Father came home Mother told him, 'We knew terror stalked the place but today it actually entered our house.'

What were we going to do about the buffalo? At a time when most of the milkmen had fled the city, the buffalo had kept us supplied with milk. It would give us milk for another four or five months before it went dry.

'Anyway, you said Kasim wanted to see me. Let me go and meet him,' said Father, his face going rather pale. Then he called softly from our veranda, 'Mr Kasim!', then called again. There was no reply. So he went out through our gate and in through theirs. He stopped at their threshold and called again 'Mr Kasim!'

Mr Kasim put his head out and asked, 'What is it?'

'I've come to see you.'

Kasim hesitated a bit before letting him in. Everyone in Chandru's house was nervously watching. Kasim's voice went on booming for a long time. Then Father too said something. When he came out, Father was sweating profusely.

'What he says is quite fair,' Father began. 'We mustn't leave the tap open all the time. Let's close it once we've collected our water.' No one responded to Father's statement. There was water in the tap for only a few minutes each day. Keeping the tap open or closed was not going to make any difference.

'Did he say anything about our buffalo?' Mother wanted to know. 'Are we supposed to beg his permission to have cattle in our house?'

'Shhh, softly,' Father warned. 'I told him we won't give it any water.'

The tap couldn't be opened at all. First Chandru and then his father tried and gave up. Kasim had closed it very tight. 'A few knocks with the hammer may do the trick,' Mother suggested. But that could invite more trouble from Kasim. So Father went to Kasim's for the second time and called, 'Mr Kasim!'

Kasim refused to come. 'Where's the hurry? I'll come tomorrow and open it for you.' Which meant that Father was expected to go and wait at his door the next morning. It was the last day for buying the month's ration of sugar. Father and Mother had been enquiring every day at the ration shop but stocks of sugar had not arrived as yet, the shopkeeper said. He had promised to give them one seer if they came on the last day at closing time. One seer was just two pounds. If they went now and caught the shopkeeper in the right mood and acknowledged receipt of six seers of sugar, they might get one seer. 'You'd better go with your father,' said Mother. So Chandru set out, walking silently with his father.

Many houses in Lancer Barracks were locked. Guard Nagabhushanam had managed to get a railway pass without a police permit and the whole family had left. Only the houses of Jafar Ali, Mannas and Kasim still had families in them.

Instead of their usual shortcut through Manohar Talkies to the ration shop, Father and Chandru now went through Charles Street and the Regimental Bazaar Police station. The dimly lit police station wore a sorry look. Like all other bright lights in Secunderabad, the mercury lamp in the police station had also been removed. The ordinary bulbs were all fitted with tiny black skirts, reminding one of the blackout of the World War years. This was a precaution against Indian air attacks. Though there were still six months left of the Standstill Agreement, Hyderabad was in the grip of a phobia. War conditions prevailed in the area.

They had to go past the Rajasthani oil store. Monda was nearly empty. The oil shop was closed. The boy from the shop who belonged to the Arya Samaj had been badly beaten by the police. Someone from Chandru's house had gone to the shop the other day and had returned without oil. The boy was there, his face horribly swollen.

Chandru walked silently with his father. To think that he used to look forward eagerly to these visits with Father to Monda until two years ago! They would discuss everything they could think of by the time they reached Monda and would meet a lot of people there as well. When Father met an acquaintance on the way, they would start talking in the middle of the road, then would keep moving out inch by inch, still engrossed in their conversation, till they finally stood on the verge of the road. Chandru would feel bored listening all the while, but it had all given him glimpses of worlds beyond his ken. Today they had walked two miles to the heart of the city but there wasn't a soul to talk to...

The man at the ration shop collected their ration card and money and went into the house next to the shop. Ten minutes later, he came out with a small packet in a bag. They would have to make do with this sugar for a whole month. Father asked the shopkeeper in Telugu if rice was available—even five seers would go a long way.

'There is some rice, very poor quality rice. But I heard you get good rice in the railway rations.'

'Oh no. It's that awful reddish rice that we get with lots of stones. Gives you diarrhea. You feel like making do with maize rotis. But somehow we never seem to get used to these rotis.'

The shopkeeper whispered, 'Hyderabad doesn't get any supply of rice or food items. The planes are bringing in only guns and tanks. That white man's plane seems to have landed in Malakpet even today.'

'Is that so?' said Father.

Not that Father didn't know. Chandru had also heard all about the Australian gun-runner Sydney Cotton who had purchased arms abroad for the Nizam's forces and had managed to smuggle them into Hyderabad under the very nose of the Indian Army. Rumour, which had at first numbered these forays as two or three, had now increased the score to dozens of times. Panic spread when it was also rumoured that he had brought in a tank by air.

There had been an incident in Bibinagar twenty miles from Secunderabad, a town chosen by Kasim Razvi for exemplary punishment. He got four Hyderabad Police trucks to carry his men there and set fire to a whole street of shops and reduced them to ashes. Houses and shops were looted. Three were killed and forty wounded, no one knew the exact number. But what really was shocking was the way the women...

So the sugar had been bought. But Father wasn't finished yet. Having come this far, he'd do well to buy a few vegetables as well. They climbed onto the platform at Monda and bought a few things from the scattered stalls there. Father then went towards the market gate. At the gate was a clock tower. There used to be two food shops there, one on either side of the entrance. One was called Bharat Bhavan, the other Sholapurwala. Bharat Bhavan had shut shop, only Sholapurwala stayed on. Father bought a sweet called sone-mithai, for six annas.

A peculiar sequence of events—Father returning from work—the house tense with the Kasim episode—Father waiting at Kasim's door, calling, 'Mr Kasim, Mr Kasim!'—the momentary stop at the closed oil shop—the ration shop owner telling them rice was no longer imported, only guns—and now here was father buying sweets! How did one link up this last fact with the rest?

Father asked the vendor for a small piece of the sweet and gave it to Chandru. As a boy, he had always waited eagerly for this moment. Now he stood there, a young man with an undergrowth of a moustache, but Father still thought it fit to get a free sweet for him.

When they left the shop Father asked him, 'How did you like it?'

'It was good.'

They met Dr Purushottam who was shutting his dispensary for the day. 'Just a minute, Mr Iyer,' he said when he saw Father. He was in the process of closing his clinic, arranging a series of vertical planks in their grooves. Only two planks remained. Father stood there for a moment, then took up a plank. Chandru held the lock. Together, they finished the boarding up and locked the place. The doctor wore his oversized trousers fastened at the waist with a necktie as he always did.

The doctor and Father walked together, talking. Chandru followed a few paces behind. The doctor was narrating his woes which by now were common to most people. His wife, son, daughter-in-law and the grandchildren had all left. They had asked him to come along, but how was he to leave the dispensary? He had a boy to help him in the clinic but the boy too had fled, so now at opening time it seemed that the doctor first got into his clinic without removing all the planks. Then he swept and dusted the room himself before removing the other planks for the public. He was beginning to feel his age, more so with this routine of boarding over and dismantling the shop-front everyday. Only the night before, a plank had fallen on his right big toe.

It was even worse at home, he said, where he had left the housekeeping to a maid, an awful woman who was feeding an army of her own at his expense in the days when everything was scarce. But he was afraid to challenge her, lest she should leave him. This was the plight of a man who had spent fifty years of his life for the sake of his family, working for them, caring for them, worrying for them. They had all gone now, leaving him to fend for himself. After all, was there any point in running away, he wondered. Would someone come and swallow them up here? Riots and disturbances had always been happening in this place. Had the whole population run away at any time? And what did these fools hope to do elsewhere? Settle down? How could they? No, they would have to return some day.

Chandru and his father walked up to Dr Purushottam's house. Once he entered it, the house seemed to swallow him. They then retraced their steps, past the railway station and the Regimental Bazaar police station. The walk had calmed then somewhat. They still hadn't spoken to each other, but the lapse didn't appear significant any more.

The May night was pleasant and balmy. The fragrance of the blossoming night-queen came in gusts through the darkness, you couldn't tell from where. The belief was that a snake was sure to be nearby wherever this sweet smell was present. But then, a snake would have its own smell, that of a raw potato. Yes, snakes did smell like that. But now there was nothing but the scent of the flowers all the way from Keyes High School to Lancer Barracks. The impartial largesse of the night-queen. Chandru wondered who had named it so aptly. This queen didn't bother in the least about matters like the country's independence or subjection.

When they reached home they found Mr Syed of Nallagutta there. He began to pepper Father with questions the moment he saw him. His tone was that of a childhood friend and he used the intimate suffix 'da' liberally. 'So we have a fool like you, do we?' he began. 'Your wife tells me your neighbour came and shouted at her. What else can it be if you don't allow him water? You seem to imagine you're still in the brahmin quarter of your village, Chattanapuram. You can't live like that here.' Then he turned upon Chandru—'So you seem to have said goodbye to your studies. I don't know why you're led by the nose by all those people. As the proverb goes a town divided is the vagrant's delight. It's their business to incite people. But why don't you have your wits about you?'

Father went straight to the kitchen without saying a word. He left the sugar and vegetables there, came back, dragged a chair beside Syed's and sat down. Syed meanwhile kept up his harangue. 'You railway people are a troublesome lot, I tell you. All those refugees have come here, fearing for their lives and leaving house and home, but it looks as if they aren't given jobs in the railways. All these Naidus and Reddys seem to be blocking them. Now you tell me, are the railways your grandfather's bequest to you? Not at all. Everything belongs to the Nizam. Is it fair that his people should be denied employment in his railways? Sheer injustice, blackguardism.'

Father cut in with, 'Now tell me how you are.'

'Oh fine,' said Syed 'No complaints. I've been made the captain of the Volunteers Corps in our locality, Nallagutta. See how honour is thrust on me? If I had just kept to Mayavaram and Cuddalore in Madras Presidency, do you think any of this would have come my way? No sir. Not at my age anyway.'

Father asked Syed if he would have something to eat.

'We've nothing but maize rotis to offer, of course. But there's brinjal to go with it. I know how much you like it.'

'I've already had some. In fact I asked your wife myself for some and then she told me about the water tap. I have opened the tap. Now don't you go blaming your neighbour for nothing. Actually it's you who lack experience in such matters.'

'How's everyone at home?' Father enquired. 'Did your son get a job?'

'Hyderabad is not like Madras, you know that. There's no dearth of jobs here. Everyone who comes here gets a job. My son is with me in the Volunteers Corps. How is it that you haven't visited us for so long?'

'I did come,' Father said, 'last week. But you were not home. You'd gone out somewhere.'

'Ah that,' said Syed. 'I'd gone to Razvi Sahib's meeting. That's what made me realise what these Congresswalas are up to. Our Nizam's PM lodged a protest with the Indian Government. Think of the people's plight when commodities that have been coming into the State all these years are suddenly stopped. He also complained against Indian planes flying over Hyderabad and do you know the sort of reply he got?'

'No, I don't,' Father said, 'No paper mentions these things, you know.'

'Now, the question we'd asked was, why are you starving our people? But in reply, they're asking us. "Why did you give 200 million rupees to Pakistan? Why do you hold all these meetings? Why do you do this? Why do you do that?" The wolf sitting in judgement over the sheep, that's what it is.'

'What's that about the 200 million?'

'Oh that. Our Nizam has lent it to Pakistan,' Syed explained. 'Look, Pakistan is a Muslim country. Isn't it natural for our Nizam to go to its help? If one Muslim doesn't help another, who will? And then, do you know what these refugees from Punjab did? They've burnt everything and ruined Pakistan before they came running to India. After all that, what right have you to question us? Who are you to ask us, "Why did you send money there? Why did you send men there?" These cowards will be the first to scamper away at the sound of a gun. None of their tricks with us. They shall be crushed.'

'Look Syed,' said Father. 'You proclaim Indian currency is not legal tender in Hyderabad, then how do you expect Indian goods to come in as usual? Credit me with some sense, will you?'

'What do we need Indian currency for? Haven't we had the Nizam's halli currency for generations here? The British had their own currency, of course, and it was trustworthy. These white Gandhi capwalas are usurping the British chair now. But how can anyone trust their money?'

'You ought to be the Nizam's minister, really.'

'And I shall be, too,' Syed said, 'Someday, certainly. I find it impossible to keep quiet when such a lot of injustice is being done. My blood boils. And... another thing... keep this to yourself... It's about these communists. We thought of them as mere scoundrels and thieves. Not at all. It is they who are now telling these whitecapwalas, "Hands off Hyderabad!" You know that? They know what these Gandhi capwalas are like. At the first shot of war between the Nizam and India, our first supporters against India will be the communists. It's all being done very secretly. Don't breathe a word to a soul.'

4

For four days now no trains had entered or left the Nizam's State of Hyderabad. That had put an end to all mail, telegrams, Indian magazines and visitors. Hyderabad had become a land-locked island. Something else had also happened, as was proclaimed by Kasim's radio next door. The Father of Pakistan, Mohammed Ali Jinnah, was dead. Hardly eight months had passed since Gandhi's death. Kasim's radio kept mourning elaborately the death of the 'Quaid-e-Azam', the supreme ruler.

The press however was extremely cautious. A Muslim journalist Shoyabullah Khan's blood had flowed and congealed on the streets of Hyderabad. His hands had been cut off and flung away on the streets for his having dared to write in the *Imroze* that it would not be a feasible proposition for Hyderabad to remain independent of India. Such sentiments coming from a Hindu journalist would have merited only a term in prison, perhaps. But how could a Muslim, an ungrateful wretch of a Muslim, write such things against the Nizam? How could a Muslim even harbour such thoughts? So he was shot dead as a warning—Beware, you treasonous vermin, you shall meet the same fate as that of the swine, beware!

But Chandru could sense a difference in the air now. Mother seemed to have felt it even before he did. The radio had given up mourning! Now it was some sort of martial music the whole day with a wild thumping of drums. There were frenzied group songs about some flag and one song proclaimed 'We got Pakistan with a smile, we'll get Hindustan fighting!'

War—was a war really on?

No one stirred out of the house. Monday was a holiday. Father's office was closed over Jinnah's death. It was on Monday evening that news of the war came. Indian troops had entered Hyderabad State from the west and southeast. A state of emergency was proclaimed in the whole state—air raid precaution measures were to be observed in all cities. No lights were to be seen at night.

Mother put two locks each on the front and back doors. There was no rice at home, no vegetables. Not even water. Going without water for another day was a frightening prospect. They had not bathed or washed. Even going to the toilet was restricted. The buffalo provided some milk, the only thing that stood between them and starvation now.

On Tuesday, however, Father went to the office to forestall any action being taken against him for not coming to work. Seven or eight people had been dismissed from the Railways for no apparent reason, all of them with twenty-eight and thirty years of service. Dismissal now would mean that he would forfeit even the tiny sum given at retirement. With no other job in sight, he would be left on the streets with his family when old age was already creeping on him.

Lancer Barracks was, to all appearances, much the same. Morris and Terence, now grown like hefty bulls, were still on the banyan tree, swinging from its hanging roots.

Chandru was about to go towards the banyan when water started to come through the tap. He ran into the house and his mother and he filled up a few big vessels.

Kasim's family next door were also collecting water. Their radio was off. The whole of the previous day and night their radio had kept up a constant boom of martial songs. It was strangely silent now.

'Did you notice?' Mother asked Chandru.

'What?'

'A lot of people seem to have come to Kasim's house.'

She was right. But when did they come? They were not there yesterday, not during the day. They must have come after dark. But why? There was no Muslim festival on at this time.

When Chandru started for the banyan tree, Mother said, 'Please don't.' He went all the same. Morris was the first to say, 'How are you?'

'Any news?' Chandru asked him.

'What about?'

'Doesn't your father go to work?'

'With no trains running he's off duty all the time.'

'My father's gone to work.'

'But your father works in an office.'

'So you really don't know anything?'

'About the fight? Nothing definite. But Indian troops have entered Hyderabad. I'm going to the city today to find out.'

Father brought the news earlier than Morris—Indian troops were advancing towards Hyderabad city from all directions. Whenever there had been pitched battles, the Nizam's army had backed away or surrendered. Those who really fought for the Nizam were the Razakars with unkempt hair and soiled shirts. They had confronted Indian tanks with brandishing swords. Two thousand of them had been mown down in just ten minutes, a vain harvest indeed. But according to Hyderabad Radio the forces of Hyderabad were advancing everywhere. They were supposed to have captured Masulipatnam.

'Did the communists fight alongside the Razakars?' Chandru asked his father.

Father was taken aback for a moment to find Chandru speaking to him. Then he said, 'I don't know. But the police and the military had been fighting them, decimating them all these years. So it's rather unlikely that they would take sides with the Razakars now.'

'Mr Syed said so, remember?'

'Oh, Syed,' said Father, 'you don't suppose the man's in his right mind, do you?'

Curfew was imposed in Secunderabad and Hyderabad. Anyone found on the streets after 6 p.m. was to be shot at sight. The announcement was couched between other bits such as 'The Nizam's forces march towards Delhi after capturing Masulipatnam on the east coast and Goa on the west coast'. 'The Indian Agent-General K.M. Munshi's residence in Bolaram is being guarded to protect him from a possible mob attack.'

Even after six in the evening, Chandru kept wandering the grounds of Lancer Barracks. It was not only the Hindu houses, the Anglo-Indian and Muslim houses were also shut, an occasional sliver of light sneaking out through the tiny gaps in the closed doors and windows. The place had already settled down for the night.

As he came out he looked at Oxford Street, a long stretch with ups and downs till it reached the Wazir Sultan buildings and was then lost to sight. The sun, now ready to plunge behind the buildings, seemed to call him. But how safe was it to follow the sun which was about to be quenched when there were fires flaming everywhere?

Chandru wanted to put his trust in the sun. His idea of a curfew was very hazy. 'Shoot at sight'—with what? A pistol? A rifle? Wouldn't the culprit run away before anyone could take aim? A man on the run may be shot on open ground or a straight road, but on these meandering lanes and bylanes? If the man entered a house, would they shoot at the house? At the front door? Through a window? Or at the roof?

Oxford Street offered little scope for finding out as policemen were rarely seen in this area. One had to go to the clock tower. But there was no policeman even at the clock tower today. The place was completely deserted, not a person was about.

But there was, or rather were, two policemen, the sole occupants of a dilapidated bus, which rattled past. One of them spotted Chandru and shouted. 'Go on, get away home!' The bus didn't slow down and was soon gone, leaving behind a smell of groundnut oil, as if a feast for a hundred had been cooked there.

Chandru returned home watching his long shadow all the way. The shadow started from his feet about ten or twelve feet long, but it seemed to have a will of its own.

Wandering all over the place. 'Don't watch your shadow, you'll grow thin.'—Who had said that? Never mind who. Anyway, shadow-watching was quite worth the risk. His shadow was dancing in front of him, trying to tell him something. But alas, in some unknown tongue. Shadow, shadow tell me true.

Chandru had a good look at neighbour Kasim's house before he went in. The window had been secured with wooden board nailed to the frame so that it couldn't be opened. One of the double doors in front had also received the same kind of reinforcement.

Chandru hadn't entered his house yet when Kasim's door opened and a man came out. He didn't see Chandru. He sat down near the wall for about a minute, then stood up. A man of around fifty, someone Chandru had never seen there before. As the man was tying his pyjama strings, his eyes fell on Chandru. He salaamed him, two very humble salaams. Then he went into the house and bolted the door. Kasim's house stood silent once more.

It was on Wednesday that the city threw off its silence. There was no news on Hyderabad Radio or war cries. It was film songs all the time. The townspeople were up and about, somewhat more than was usual. There weren't many policemen about and those that were around looked rather shaken. People could be seen everywhere, standing about in groups, their talk open and free. Passenger-riding on bicycles was prohibited but was now seen everywhere even near the police stations. Police stations for that matter appeared deserted. The Regimental Bazaar police station usually had a permanent display of swords and firearms which could be seen from the road. These had now been removed.

Were there so many people still left in the city, one wondered looking at the crowds. Only men were seen out on the streets, Hindus. Chandru went to the railway station. The buses weren't plying. They were all parked in a row. Red-shirted porters enjoyed a game of dice in the shade with squares drawn on the ground. At the Nizam's customs booth, the tall woman sat alone with the door ajar. SPG School and a few shops in front of the station were closed. Two Irani restaurants were open, a gramaphone played in each.

Chandru walked along Station Road, with the KEM Hospital on one side and the refugee shacks on the other. Smoke curled up from many of the shacks. Few city people passed this way. And the refugees didn't seem too eager to communicate with others. Nor did they bother about what was happening in the rest of the world. Their wash, also in tatters, was spread on the fence of the hospital. Their pitiable clothes and possessions went well with their sunken cheeks and eyes. A year had gone by since they first came to live in these three-foot bamboo shanties.

Chandru found a refugee looking him straight in the eye and smiling. If he had even a single anna on him, Chandru would have bought some snacks from him. But now what could he do in return for that smile? Nothing.

In Monda Market, the shops were still closed, but there were lots of people moving about, talking. Such a scene would not have met one's eyes two days ago. Not that anybody knew anything specific even now. But one thing was certain—Indian troops were out to punish the Nizam. All troubles were about to end. Maybe in a week's time, maybe two weeks, or a month at the most.

Despite this new surge of hope, the city was restrained. Order was kept, the law was obeyed. Perhaps the people were being very cautious because the present turn in the affairs seemed too good to be true.

After a day spent visiting every part of Secunderabad, Chandru returned home in the evening. There was some bustle and life in Lancer Barracks as well now. Even Kasim's door was open. Though Kasim himself was not to be seen, lots of other people, old and young, were there. Their expressions showed a readiness to agree with whatever you said. The men kept salaaming everyone who passed by.

Once again, it was the Railways that had reliable and detailed information. Indian troops were advancing on the Suryapet-Hyderabad road without meeting any resistance. The confrontations, when they did occur, had an element of farce about them, like the one at Aurangabad.

There a college professor had tried to stop an armoured vehicle, with a hundred students armed with sticks. The first round of firing shattered twenty students and the rest just ran for their lives.

When taken into custody, the professor went on hysterically shouting 'Azad Hyderabad Zindabad!' The Razakars of Hyderabad were already a spent force and had ceased to be a source of worry.

The real cause for worry now was the condition of thousands of political prisoners in the State's fifteen-odd prisons. What had the Razakars done with them? As for the radio at home the light came on, and a hum like wasps. Nothing could be expected of it any more. So Father went and stood out on the front veranda and called out loudly: 'Kasim! Mr Kasim!' After the fourth or fifth call, an old man opened the door and peeped out. 'Kasim is not in town. But I am here to do whatever you want.'

'I would like to have your radio,' Father said.

'The radio?... Let me find out.' The old man disappeared. By now the whole family had assembled beside Father on the veranda. The old man came out again and said, 'I'm told it's out of order.'

'How? It was all right yesterday.'

While the old man smiled sheepishly, a female voice from behind him said, 'You're welcome to have a look at it. Take it if it works.'

Chandru said, 'Let me go and see.' There were no comments. Chandru vaulted the wall between their two gardens and reached Kasim's door. The old man stood aside to let him in.

When he stepped into the house, Chandru was confused. He felt the vein on his forehead throb. Deeper in the house, he found it suffocating, with swarms of people everywhere and an overpowering stench. Pyari Begum was there, too.

The old man said, 'Here it is,' and pointed at the radio. The room was dark and unlit. Chandru looked round. Then Kasim's wife flicked a switch. As the light flooded the room, the plight of this cringing mass of humanity seemed even more pitiable. The old women pulled on their veils. Chandru switched on the radio. Nothing happened. Not even the light came on. Chandru turned the knobs. While turning the last knob, he happened to slide the radio a little. Something caught his attention. There were pieces of fine broken glass under the set. His suspicions were now aroused, and he turned the set round and looked at the back. It was a valves set and he found two broken. It was impossible for them to be broken like that unless someone had done it on purpose. The old man stood by with a meek look and Kasim's wife glowered at him. Chandru vaulted the wall again and was home. The lights went out in Kasim's house and Mother said 'Well?'

'It's no use.' Chandru said.

'Why, it used to play so well.'

A grass cart came in the morning. A hawker brought guavas. And after a long time, a woman came selling corncobs. A beggar sold them half a seer of rice. There was quite a crowd today on the street, even the big shops were open. Vendors were selling fresh vegetables. Tailors and barber shops were also open. A barber known to Chandru called out to him. 'I don't have the money,' said Chandru.

'It's all right. Pay me tomorrow.' And even when Chandru said 'I'm going to have a bath when I go home,' the barber put some hair oil on his hair and powdered his face. He seemed to be in high spirits today. There was a newspaper lying in his shop, from Bezwada. If only he'd learnt Telugu, thought Chandru wistfully, he could have now read it and got some news.

For there was a lot to know. The Nizam's commanders had made it clear that no more fighting was possible. For one thing the Nizam's forces were never a match for the Indian army with its vast numbers and weapons. For another there were no fortresses or garrison towns in the state to stop the attacking army and compel them to give battle. The south-eastern part of the state was a plain for the most part and afforded no protection against the onslaught of the Indian tanks. The question now was, what was Pakistan going to do to help the Nizam? It was evident that it couldn't do much. A complaint was to be lodged with the UN, not directly but through a member country which would obviously be Pakistan. The Nizam's representative to the UN, a Nawab, was said to have taken a sizeable quantity of gold and other valuables from the state treasury out of the country. Was this true? Possibly.

It was everyone for himself now. Save your own skin.

The people's guesses about future events could no longer be dismissed as childish—a battle might be fought in this very place in another month, no ten days, possibly even a week's time.

There were fewer policemen out today than yesterday. Ninety-five per cent of Hyderabad's police were Muslims. Muslims were not to be seen anywhere today.

But there were Muslims who couldn't help being seen, hundreds of them, all refugees. They had made the pavements of the streets their home. They were highly visible, in the centre of the town, near the railway station, opposite the main hospital, by an old Christian church. Cooking smoke still curled out of their log huts. God knew if they had had anything to eat but they went on preparing snack-food and selling it to the Muslim restaurants. With the money, they bought gram flour and oil in the black market and prepared some more food. Did they eat a little of what they made? But then, looking at them, was this the look of people who ate? Chandru was looking for the refugee who had smiled at him last evening. No, he wasn't there. But there were others, quite a few of them, all of them very very calm. While the whole town was agog, these people just didn't have it in them to feel anything. It was not the patient wait for something to happen, but the indifference of those past caring, past caring even for their children whose clothes were among those drying on the hospital fence.

In Kingsway, groups of people stood talking in the middle of the street. The house of the socialist leader of Secunderabad, Mahadev Singh, was somewhere nearby.

He had been in jail for eight months now. His family was allowed to meet him only three times in all those eight months. For two days now, they had been trying to meet him, or at least to find out if he was still alive. New information was forthcoming, although it was known that political prisoners from prisons in other towns were to be brought to Hyderabad Central Jail. Perhaps they were already here. In Gulbarga, the Razakars had entered the jail and beaten up the Congress prisoners. One had died. Now that the Razakars had reason enough to be incensed, who could imagine how they would react?

The only vehicles on the streets were bicycles and tongas. But the tongas were mostly empty. It looked as if no one had the patience or need to engage a tonga.

The food shops were all empty now. Everything had been sold out in an hour. Betel leaves were selling at an exorbitant four rupees a hundred. Other tradespeople were not greatly bothered about sales. After waiting in the shops for a while, most of them had left their plumped up bolsters to have a chat with other shopowners.

'Police action' was the term All India Radio used to describe the entry of Indian forces into Hyderabad. The troops were still advancing, they claimed. Radio Hyderabad suddenly asked its listeners to stand by for an important announcement at 4.30 p.m. This was repeated every ten minutes, the interval being filled by playing recorded music. But this announcement did little to increase the general pitch of excitement which was high even otherwise. Long before 4.30.p.m., it was known that the Indian troops had reached Bongir. Just thirty miles to Hyderabad.

At 4.30 came a cryptic annuouncement: 'A royal proclamation will be read out by the Nizam himself over the radio at 7.30 p.m.' The curfew had ceased to matter. The whole city, that is its male half, was out on the streets by 6.30 p.m. There were a few bold women as well, vendors of vegetables, fried peas or gram-patti. Such was their faith in the people's honourable proclivities. To be sure, the city and its people had kept peace without the benefit of any reminders from the authorities for four days now, since military action had been initiated.

More people listened to the Nizam's *firman* from the streets than from within their houses. They had been waiting for some time with every radio in every house and shop set at full volume when the Nizam's voice came over clearly, in English:

> 'We are aware that our land and our subjects have been experiencing extremely unusual conditions in the recent past. In order to alleviate this without further delay, certain measures have been undertaken by us. The president of our Executive Council and his colleagues have tendered their resignations this morning. We have decided that the State of Hyderabad shall accede to the Indian Union. In pursuance of this our first instruction had been to our troops and para-military forces to cease all hostilities against the Indian armed forces. An order had also been issued to implement such measures as

> shall lead to the installation of a civil administration. In the interim period, the governance of the state shall rest with the representative appointed by the Government of India.
>
> As a step towards normalisation, all political prisoners in the state have been ordered to be released. The curfew and other precautionary measures which were brought into force at the beginning of this week stand cancelled with immediate effect. It is our hope that our subjects shall undertake it as their duty to ensure that our State continues to function in a manner not detrimental to its ancient prestige and glory. It behoves us to express our gratitude to our friend, Chakravarti Rajagopalachari, the Indian Governor-General and Mr K.M. Munshi who had been with us as the Indian Agent-General for the assistance rendered towards arriving at an amicable settlement and avoiding a grave situation.'

The broadcast ended. Those who had been listening didn't evince any undue excitement or enthusiasm. A few isolated cries of 'Jai Hind!' and 'State Congress Zindabad!' broke the silence but failed to be taken up, and died away. Strangely, that was when, for the first time in those four days, Chandru felt a snake of fear.

As if to reassure him, a general buzz rose from the crowd—there had been no mention in the Nizam's speech about the Razakars or their leader Razvi, people pointed out. Didn't the Indian Government consider them culpable? Was there going to be no retribution for their brutal and barbaric deeds? What about those countless people who fell victims to the Razakar atrocities? Had their blood been shed in vain, their lives been sacrificed for nothing?

Others spoke in a different vein. How could one expect the Nizam to refer to all that? He could only mention the vital points. Anyway Hyderabad had finally acceded to the Indian Union. So it was now up to the Indian Government to take further action. Something must be afoot even now. It would be known tomorrow, perhaps.

Kasim's door stayed shut. The windows in front and at the back were all closed. How long could some thirty or forty people live in two rooms depending on a ventilator on the high roof for air? History has it that in Calcutta about two centuries ago, 146 people were shut in like that and 123 of them had died in a single night.

Mother was sound asleep. Everyone was sound asleep. After all, they had spent the whole year here and had not run away to save their skins, though many had done so. Tomorrow was to be the dawn of a new era. An era that knew no fear, no horror, no terror. Perhaps. Sleep eluded Chandru and he came out. The night was pleasant. Time for Secunderabad's second monsoon, the season of the fugitive rains. There would be rain at night and the sun all day, making you wonder if it had rained at all. It was on a day like this that Nasir Ali Khan had first invited him to cricket practice thus acknowledging him as a player and a friend. What was Nasir doing now? Did sleep elude him as well? What if he had lost his father? Was it his father, by any chance, who had led those two thousand Razakars to the massacre?

He went to the banyan tree. He had come to the banyan tree at midnight once before, when there had been the sound of distant music in the air. There were no sounds tonight, only the crickets. What time was it? How long before daybreak?

Chandru went round both rows of Lancer Barracks. Of the twenty-four houses, half were dark because they were unoccupied. The rest had adapted themselves to darkness after months of going without light. Did it mean that there was no one in these houses who needed a night lamp? No child, no sick person, no student? It was merely that the happenings in the land had seeped into its homes, insidiously altering the lives of people.

Someone was coming every night to Krishnaswamy's house just to sleep there and keep an eye on things. He seemed to have set his alarm for now. It rang when Chandru walked past the house and then stopped. Chandru felt his legs ache. But that was not entirely unexpected after all the walking he had done in the last two days, walking aimlessly, limitlessly.

It won't be long now to sunrise, he thought. This calm was the stillness of the night's last moments. In the hushed silence, he began to hear a muffled roar like a noise coming from the bottom of a well. To be so faint on such a still night, the source had to be at least a mile away.

The noise was heard again and again. From the direction of the railway station. Suddenly there was a flare on the horizon and it threw a red glow. The calm of four days was shattered.

Barely conscious of what he was doing, Chandru ran towards the station, mesmerised by the red streaks on the horizon. Once he reached Regimental Bazar he knew what had caused the glow and the screams. Right in front of the police station, two groups fought with sticks and brickbats.

Chandru ran towards the mob with no thought for the consequences. It was just here that a riot had started once earlier—the same flour mill, the same tailor's shop. The doors of all the shops and houses in the street were closed now. It must have been the terrified screams of the women and children that Chandru had heard first.

Suddenly the people began to run in all directions, and the whole mob dissolved away, as if by magic. They disappeared down the surrounding lanes.

Even as Chandru wondered what had caused this, he knew the reason. A shot was heard—someone firing at someone else somewhere. Chandru ran through a lane, He found the whole neighbourhood awake. People stood outside. It was a predominantly Hindu locality. A lot of people had fled the town but a number still remained. There was no more need for them to cringe with fear. But the sight of them standing there made Chandru grow cold. He went through the twisting lanes at a half-run and reached the railway station. In front of those Irani restaurants where the gramophones had played even yesterday was a huge bonfire, the flames reaching twenty feet or more.

Things from the shop were being thrown into the fire, tables and chairs, cooking coal and firewood. A dozen people kept throwing crockery into the fire, the crash feeding the frenzy of the crowd of onlookers. This had been the flare of fire in the sky, visible as far as Chandru's house.

Chandru's fears lay centred elsewhere, because in these shops he knew that after an interval of a few days, new tables and chairs would be bought and business would go on as before. Since the same places were being attacked time and again in every riot in Regimental Bazaar, these attacks couldn't have been entirely unanticipated. The real horrors must be happening elsewhere.

Chandru ran on and turned at Station Road. At first every thing appeared dark, but the night lamps of the hospital shed some light on the street and slowly, as his eyes grew accustomed to the dark, the picture emerged. What he had feared had happened. The refugee shacks had been razed to the ground. Not a single one remained. The street was savagely strewn with broken pieces of pots and cooking pans, and with clothes, vegetables and foodstuff trodden underfoot. Street dogs roamed the place. Of the hundreds there even the evening before, not a person remained. They must have been attacked a few hours ago. Poor men and women, they had been living in peace there. Where could they all have vanished, without a trace? This time round, did the refugees take away anything with them?—not that they had anything to take away!

There were sudden cries of 'Run, *run!*' A crowd was rushing in from the station. Even in the dark, even in that moment of crisis, this crowd had managed to recognise the community to which Chandru belonged. And they were urging him to run along with them and hide himself. There was probably another crowd behind, driving these people on. But it wouldn't be long before they met the same fate as the refugees.

Chandru ran towards the hospital. The huge doors of the hospital were all locked. At least twenty people ran with him. A sleepless night for all was the momentary thought that flashed through his mind.

He soon reached Monda. There was rioting in Monda as well. Sticks and stones flew in all directions. A part of the crowd had made a bonfire of cane baskets. The people ran about like black ghosts in the light of the fire. Their screams were not human either. Chandru ran towards the Islamia High School. There seemed to be people behind him, chasing him. Islamia School again, he thought, the same place where he had once been attacked.

Another mob came and ran on to the other side of the street. But how could one be sure that it was a Hindu group? They carried lighted torches. Chandru slipped into an alleyway by the side of the school. The mob with the torches spotted him and followed him with cries of 'Get him! Get him!'

Chandru climbed the wall of a house and jumped in. In a few seconds he heard the crowd run past the spot shouting, 'Get the bastard! Kill him!' They ran down the lane, rattling the doors and windows with their sticks.

In the house in which Chandru found himself, everyone was awake. With their instant recognition of his community came fear, and they shrank from him. It was just one of the thousand poor Muslim houses which had only one kerosene lamp to light the place. Three or four men; three or four women; three or four children; the ubiquitous old woman.

Together those three men could have killed him. But fear had sucked them dry. The place stank sharply. Before Chandru could get a hold on himself, something happened.

The people in the house had obviously discussed this eventuality and had prepared for it in advance. From among the group of women, a girl of about sixteen came forward and stood before Chandru. She said, 'Please spare us, I implore you.' Even as she spoke, she started to unbutton her dress. She took off her long kameez. In a second she had untied the knots of her pyjama strings, and now she stood before him naked. Even in the dim light, one could count the ribs sticking out of her emaciated body.

Chandru let out an anguished cry: 'No, *no*!' His head swam. He felt sick as the bitter gorge rose in his throat. He swallowed it down, turned and ran to the wall and jumped out. Once in the street, he ran like a person possessed. Even the burnt-down shacks of the refugees had not affected him so. But this girl—and his first glimpse of a naked female body—had devastated him. She had abased herself and, by her act, had reduced him to nothing. Such self-abasement for the sake of her family—she herself was no more than a child. It seemed that in this world no one was exempt from degradation, not even children. This, *this* was the price they had to pay for their survival.

To think that he was the cause for this depravity! How was he to rid himself of the stain? Would he ever be able to?

As he ran on, he grew dimly aware of the first streaks of dawn.